The ANCIENT PERSIANS

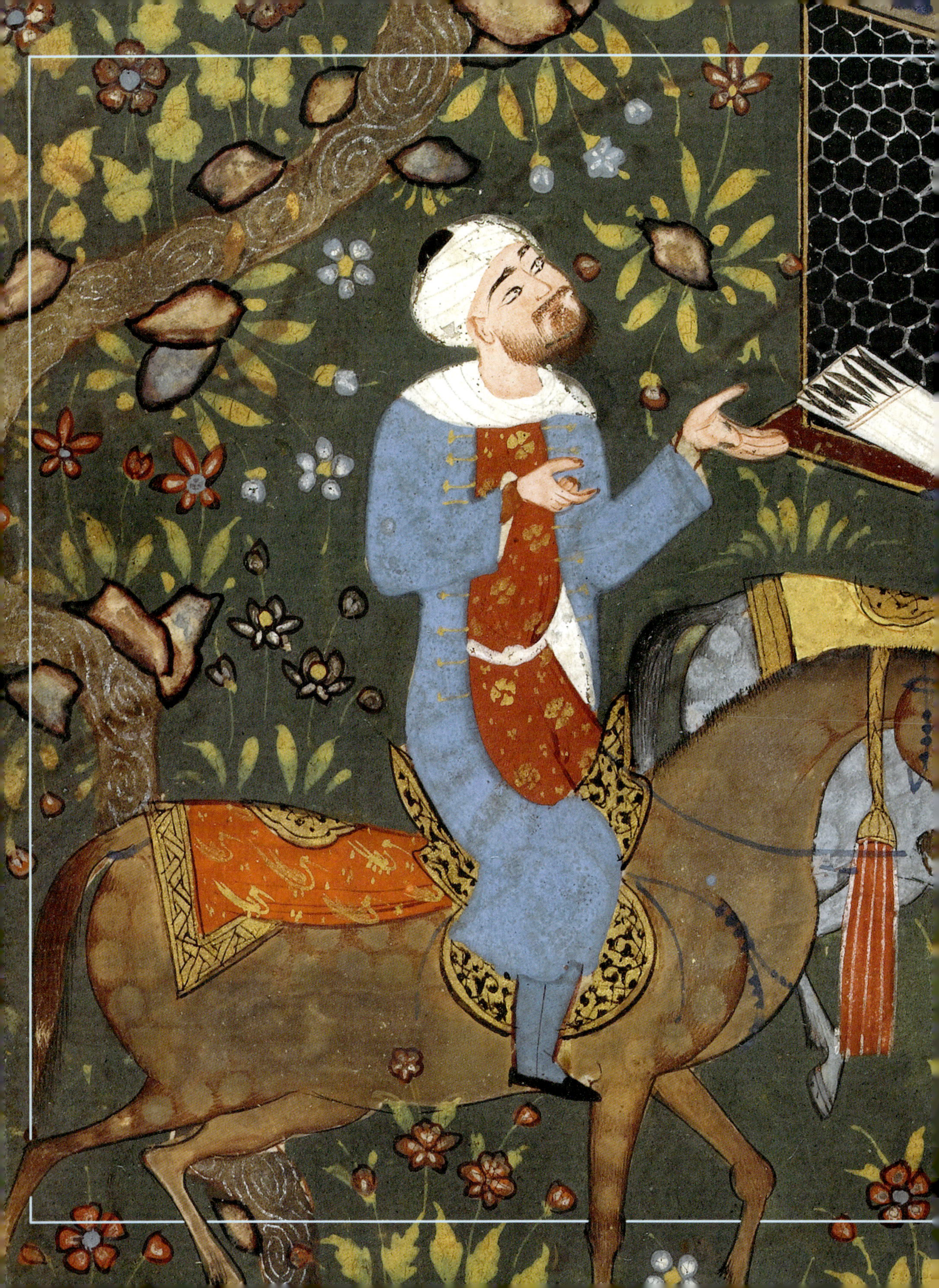

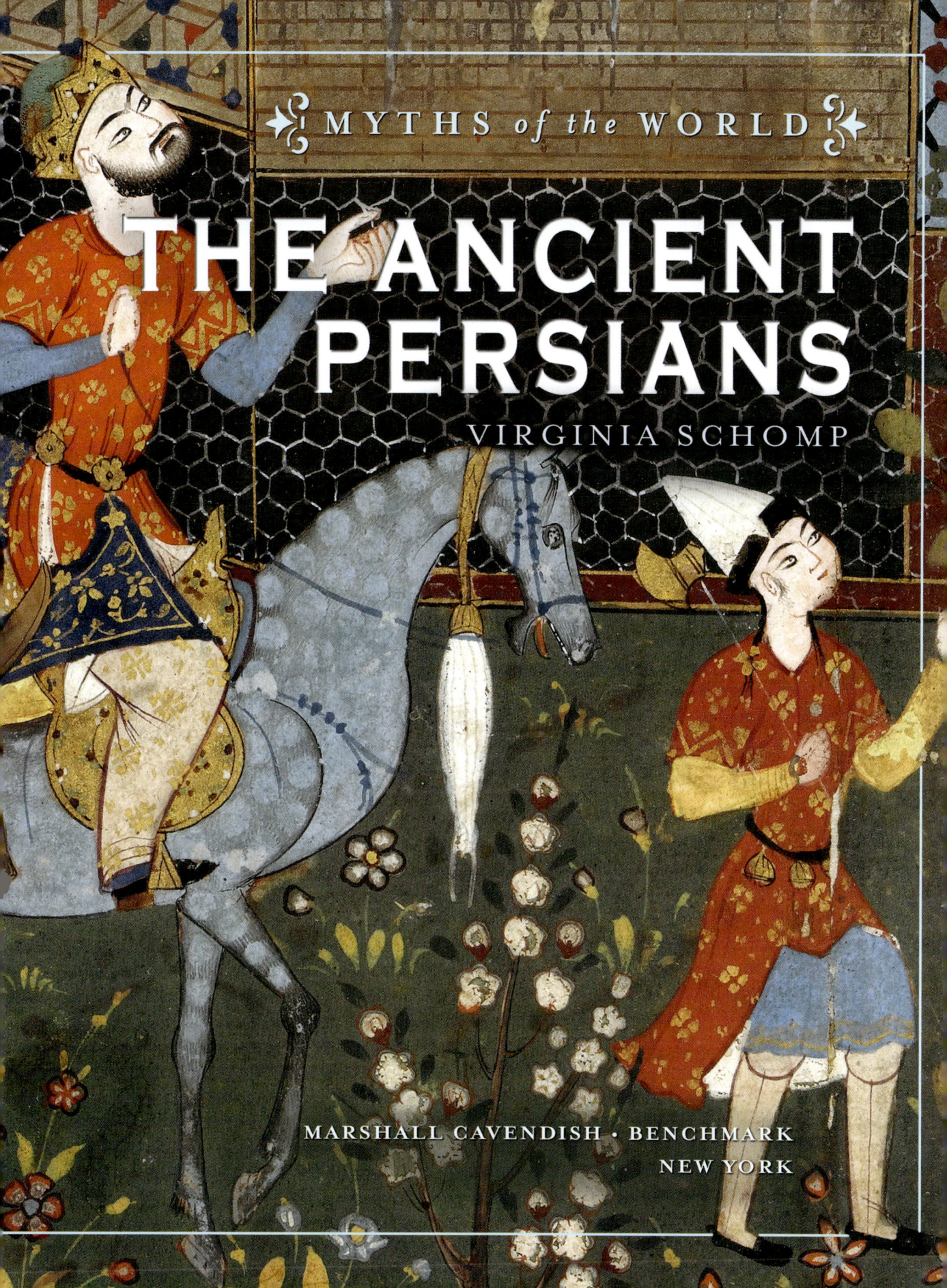

MYTHS of the WORLD

THE ANCIENT PERSIANS

VIRGINIA SCHOMP

MARSHALL CAVENDISH • BENCHMARK
NEW YORK

~ *For Savannah Adriana Kerr* ~

The author would like to thank Dr. Jamsheed K. Choksy, Professor of Central Eurasian Studies, History, and India Studies and Adjunct Professor of Religious Studies, Indiana University, for his valuable comments and careful reading of the manuscript.

Benchmark Books Marshall Cavendish 99 White Plains Road Tarrytown, New York 10591 www.marshallcavendish.us Text copyright © 2010 by Marshall Cavendish Corporation All rights reserved. No part of this book may be reproduced or utilized in any form or by any means electronic or mechanical, including photocopying, recording, or by any information storage and retrieval system, without permission from the copyright holders. All Internet sites were available and accurate when this book was sent to press. LIBRARY OF CONGRESS CATALOGING-IN-PUBLICATION DATA Schomp, Virginia. The ancient Persians / Virginia Schomp. p. cm. — (Myths of the world) Includes bibliographical references and index. Summary: "A retelling of several important ancient Persian myths, with background information describing the history, geography, belief systems, and customs of the ancient Persians"—Provided by publisher. ISBN 978-0-7614-4218-9 1. Iran—History—To 640—Juvenile literature. 2. Zoroastrianism—Juvenile literature. 3. Firdawsi. Shahnamah—Adaptations. I. Firdawsi. Shahnamah. English. Selections. II. Title. DS254.75.S346 2009 935—dc22 2009011876

EDITOR: Joyce Stanton ART DIRECTOR: Anahid Hamparian
PUBLISHER: Michelle Bisson SERIES DESIGNER: Michael Nelson

Images provided by Rose Corbett Gordon, Art Editor of Mystic CT, from the following sources: Cover: Stapleton Collection/Corbis Back cover: The Art Archive/Alfredo Dagli Orti Pages 1, 24 top, 36, 82, 84, 85: Private Collection/Bridgeman Art Library; pages 2–3, 7, 10–11: Réunion des Musées Nationaux/Art Resource, NY; pages 6, 55: Burstein Collection/Corbis; pages 8, 47: Victoria & Albert Museum/Bridgeman Art Library; page 9: The British Library/The Image Works; page 12: Musée des Arts Decoratifs, Paris/Bridgeman Art Library/Getty Images; pages 14, 50, 51, 53 bottom: Roland & Sabrina Michaud/Woodfin Camp & Associates; page 16: Alinari Archives/The Image Works; page 18: The Art Archive/Gianni Dagli Orti; page 19: (c)The Trustees of the British Museum. All rights reserved; page 20: The Art Archive/Corbis; page 22: The Art Archive/Palace of Chihil Soutoun Isfahan/Gianni Dagli Orti; page 24 bottom: Werner Forman/Art Resource, NY; page 26: Image copyright (c)The Metropolitan Museum/Art Resource, NY; page 27: (c) The Trustees of the British Museum/Art Resource, NY; pages 28–29: British Library/HIP/Art Resource, NY; pages 30, 32: The Art Archive/Museum of Anatolian Civilizations Ankara/Gianni Dagli Orti; pages 33, 45, 89: Corbis; page 35: Biblioteca Reale, Turin/Bridgeman Art Library; pages 38, 64: Edinburgh University Library/Bridgeman Art Library/With kind permission of the University of Edinburgh; pages 40, 42: Topkapi Palace Museum, Istanbul/Bridgeman Art Library; pages 43, 48, 78, 80: The Granger Collection, NY; pages 49, 58, 60, 73: Stapleton Collection/Corbis; page 53 top: The Art Archive/Archaeological Museum Teheran/Gianni Dagli Orti; page 56: Nationalmuseum, Stockholm, Sweden/Bridgeman Art Library; pages 57, 88 top: Topham/The Image Works; page 63 top: Real Monasterio de El Escorial, Spain/Bridgeman Art Library; page 63 bottom: The Art Archive/Harper Collins Publishers; page 65: SEF/Art Resource, NY; page 67: Smithsonian Institution/Corbis; pages 68, 70: Bildarchiv Preussischer Kulturbesitz/Art Resource, NY; page 71: The Art Archive/Musée Condé Chantilly/Gianni Dagli Orti; page 72: Institute of Oriental Studies, St. Petersburg, Russia/Bridgeman Art Library; page 74: Royal Asiatic Society, London/Bridgeman Art Library; page 76: The Pierpont Morgan Library/Art Resource, NY; pages 83, 88 bottom: The Art Archive; page 86: Fitzwilliam Museum, University of Cambridge/Bridgeman Art Library; page 87: Brian Wilson/Ancient Art & Architecture Collection Ltd.

Printed in Malaysia
135642

Front cover: Miniature painting of a nobleman on horseback, created in the late eighteenth century
Half-title page: A painted tile shows a princely hunter with a hawk.
Title page: The sixth-century Persian king Anushirvan rides with his vizier, or chief adviser, in this miniature painted in the 1500s in Shiraz.
Back cover: A camel and its handler, part of a wall sculpture in a palace at Persepolis

CONTENTS

THE MAGIC *of* MYTHS 6

Part 1
MEET THE ANCIENT PERSIANS
AT THE CROSSROADS 13
THE GLORIES OF PERSIA 17
KINGS, NOBLES, AND COMMONERS 21
THE TEACHINGS OF ZARATHUSTRA 23
THE SACRED FIRE 25

Part 2
TIMELESS TALES OF ANCIENT PERSIA
THE ORIGINS OF THE WORLD AND HUMANS: *Ahura Mazda and the Good Creation* 31
TALES FROM THE *SHAHNAMEH*: *The First Earthly Kings* 41
THE GOLDEN AGE: *Yima Saves the World* 51
GOOD TRIUMPHS OVER EVIL: *Zahhak the Serpent King* 59
MYTHICAL CREATURES: *Rostam and His Marvelous Horse* 69
THE FOUNDING OF ZOROASTRIANISM: *The Life of Zarathustra* 79

GLOSSARY 86
ANCIENT PERSIAN WRITING AND TEXTS 87
TO FIND OUT MORE 90
SELECTED BIBLIOGRAPHY 92
NOTES ON QUOTATIONS 93
INDEX 94

THE MAGIC *of* MYTHS

EVERY ANCIENT CULTURE HAD ITS MYTHS. These timeless tales of gods and heroes give us a window into the beliefs, values, and practices of people who lived long ago. They can make us think about the BIG QUESTIONS that have intrigued humankind down through the ages: questions about human nature, the meaning of life, and what happens after death. On top of all that, myths are simply great stories that are lots of fun to read.

What makes a story a myth? Unlike a narrative written by a particular author, a myth is a traditional story that has been handed down from generation to generation, first orally and later in written form. Nearly all myths tell the deeds of gods, goddesses, and other divine and semidivine beings. These age-old tales were once widely accepted as true and sacred. Their primary purpose was to explain the mysteries of life and the origins of a society's customs, institutions, and religious rituals.

It is sometimes hard to tell the difference between a myth and a

Above: The Persian hero Rostam confronts a company of demons.

heroic legend. Both myths and legends are traditional stories that may include extraordinary elements such as gods, spirits, magic, and monsters. Both may be partly based on real events in the distant past. However, the main characters in legends are usually mortals rather than divine beings. Another key difference is that legends are basically exciting action stories, while myths almost always express deeper meanings or truths.

Mythology (the whole collection of myths belonging to a society) played an important role in ancient cultures. In very early times, people created myths to explain the awe-inspiring, uncontrollable forces of nature, such as thunder, lightning, darkness, drought, and death. Even after science began to develop more rational explanations for these mysteries, myths continued to provide comforting answers to the many questions that could never be fully resolved. People of nearly all cultures have asked the same basic questions about the world around them. That is

A prince and his courtiers enjoy a day in the countryside.

why myths from different times and places can be surprisingly similar. For example, the people of almost every ancient society told stories about the creation of the world, the origins of gods and humans, and the afterlife.

Mythology's other roles have included providing instruction, inspiration, and entertainment. Traditional tales offer a way for the members of a society to express their fundamental beliefs and values and pass them down to future generations. The tales help preserve memories of a civilization's past glories and hold up examples of ideal human qualities and conduct. Finally, these imaginative stories have provided enjoyment to countless listeners and readers from ancient times through today.

The MYTHS OF THE WORLD series explores the mythology of some of history's greatest civilizations. Each book opens with a brief look at the culture that created the myths, including its geographical setting, political history, government, society, and religious beliefs. Next comes the fun part: the stories themselves. We have based our retellings of the myths selected for these books on a variety of traditional sources. The new versions are fun and easy to read. At the same time, we have strived to remain true to the spirit of the ancient tales, preserving their magic, their mystery, and the special ways of speech and avenues of thought that made each culture unique.

As you read the myths, you will come across sidebars, or text boxes,

Above: A man with a pet cheetah demonstrates the ancient sport of falconry, or hunting with a trained bird.

highlighting topics related to each story's characters or themes. The sidebars in *The Ancient Persians* include quoted passages from books, poems, and prayers dating back hundreds or thousands of years. The sources for the excerpts are given in the Notes on Quotations on page 93. You will find lots of other useful material at the back of the book as well, including information on ancient Persian writing and texts, a glossary of difficult terms, suggestions for further reading, and more. Finally, the stories are illustrated with both ancient and modern paintings, sculptures, and other works of art inspired by mythology. These images can help us better understand the spirit of the myths and the way a society's traditional tales have influenced other cultures through the ages.

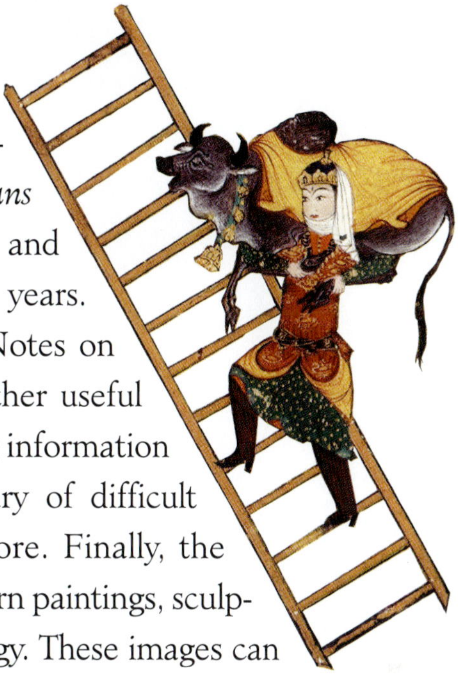

Now it is time to begin our adventures in ancient Persia. We hope that you will enjoy this journey to a land of awesome heavenly beings, horrible demons, and superhuman heroes. Most of all, we hope that the sampling of stories and art in this book will inspire you to further explorations of the magical world of mythology.

ABOUT THE PERSIAN MYTHS

The myths that we call "Persian" are actually "Iranian." As we will see in the pages that follow, the Persians were originally one group of people among several different groups who lived in ancient Iran. Those peoples shared many of the same religious beliefs and myths. In time the Persians became the dominant power in the region. They recorded the ancient Iranian tales in Persian languages. That is how the stories in this book, which really belong to all the ancient peoples of Iran, came to be called "Persian myths."

Above: A slave girl carries a cow up a ladder, in a scene from a twelfth-century Persian poem.

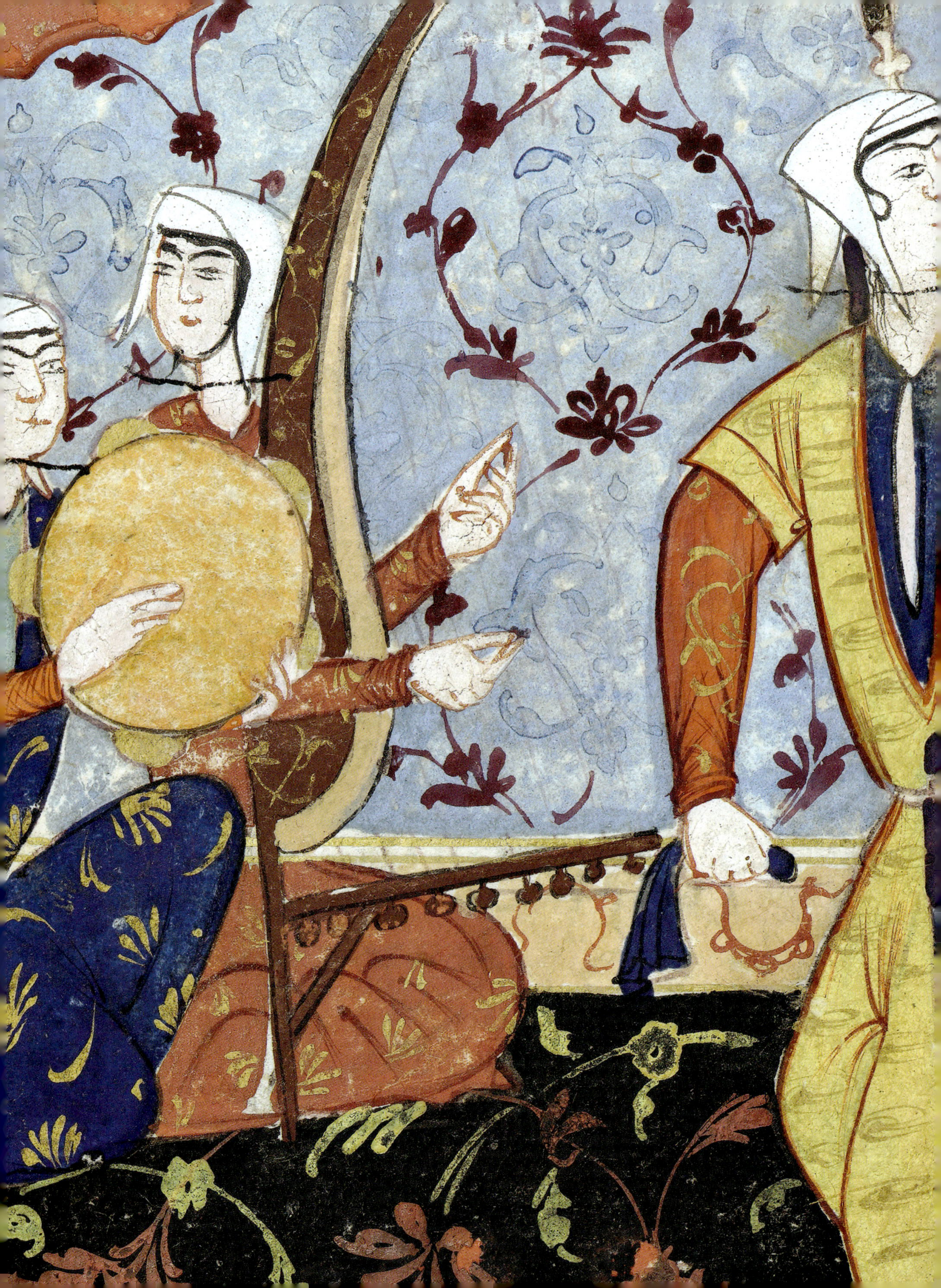

Part 1
MEET *the* ANCIENT PERSIANS

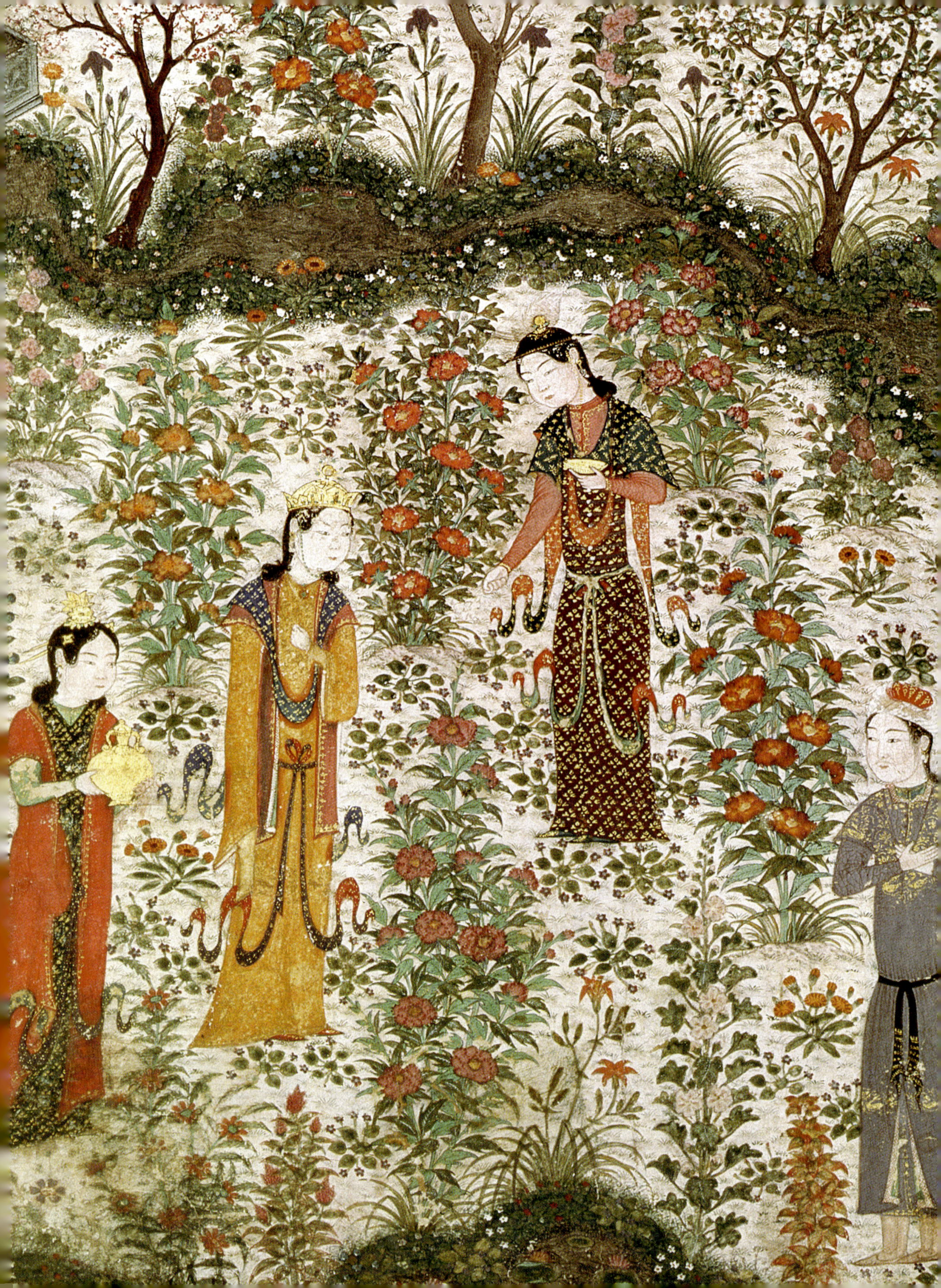

At the CROSSROADS

THE PRESENT-DAY NATION OF IRAN SITS AT THE HEART OF the Middle East. Until recently, people of the Western world called this country by a different name: *Persia*. In ancient times the Persians built the largest empire that the world had ever seen, stretching over most of Asia and parts of Europe and Africa.

The homeland of the ancient Persians was rugged and unforgiving. Iran is one of the driest, most mountainous places on earth. The central part of the country is a vast plateau consisting mainly of barren plains and salt deserts. Surrounding the plateau are towering mountain ranges. The Zagros Mountains run more than 600 miles (966 kilometers) along the shores of the Persian Gulf and Arabian Sea. The Alborz Mountains rise from a narrow coastal plain lining the shores of the salty Caspian Sea.

There are no major river systems in Iran. The only navigable river is the Karun, which flows from the Zagros Mountains to the Persian

Opposite: The Persians planted beautiful irrigated gardens in the midst of their parched homeland.

Previous page: A group of women enjoy music and dancing, in a sixteenth-century Persian painting.

Plants and trees struggle to survive in a rocky Persian landscape.

Gulf. In the early spring, many other small rivers and streams form from snow melting in the mountain ranges. The waters flow from the mountains into the central plateau, draining into saltwater lakes. Within a few weeks or months, most of the rivers and lakes dry up in the blistering summer heat.

Geography played a major role in Persian history and culture. Because of its central location, the country was an important trade link between the Western and Eastern worlds. The people of western Persia had frequent contacts with the ancient Greeks and Romans. Those in eastern Persia were influenced more by the ancient Indians and other Asian peoples. In turn, neighboring peoples absorbed many Persian ideas and beliefs.

Geography also helped shape Persian mythology. Many of the traditional tales of Persia take place in a land of dusty plains and towering mountains. In "Ahura Mazda and the Good Creation" on page 31, we will learn how the mountains and other land features were formed during the first great battle between the forces of good and evil.

THE PERSIAN EMPIRE, AROUND 500 BCE

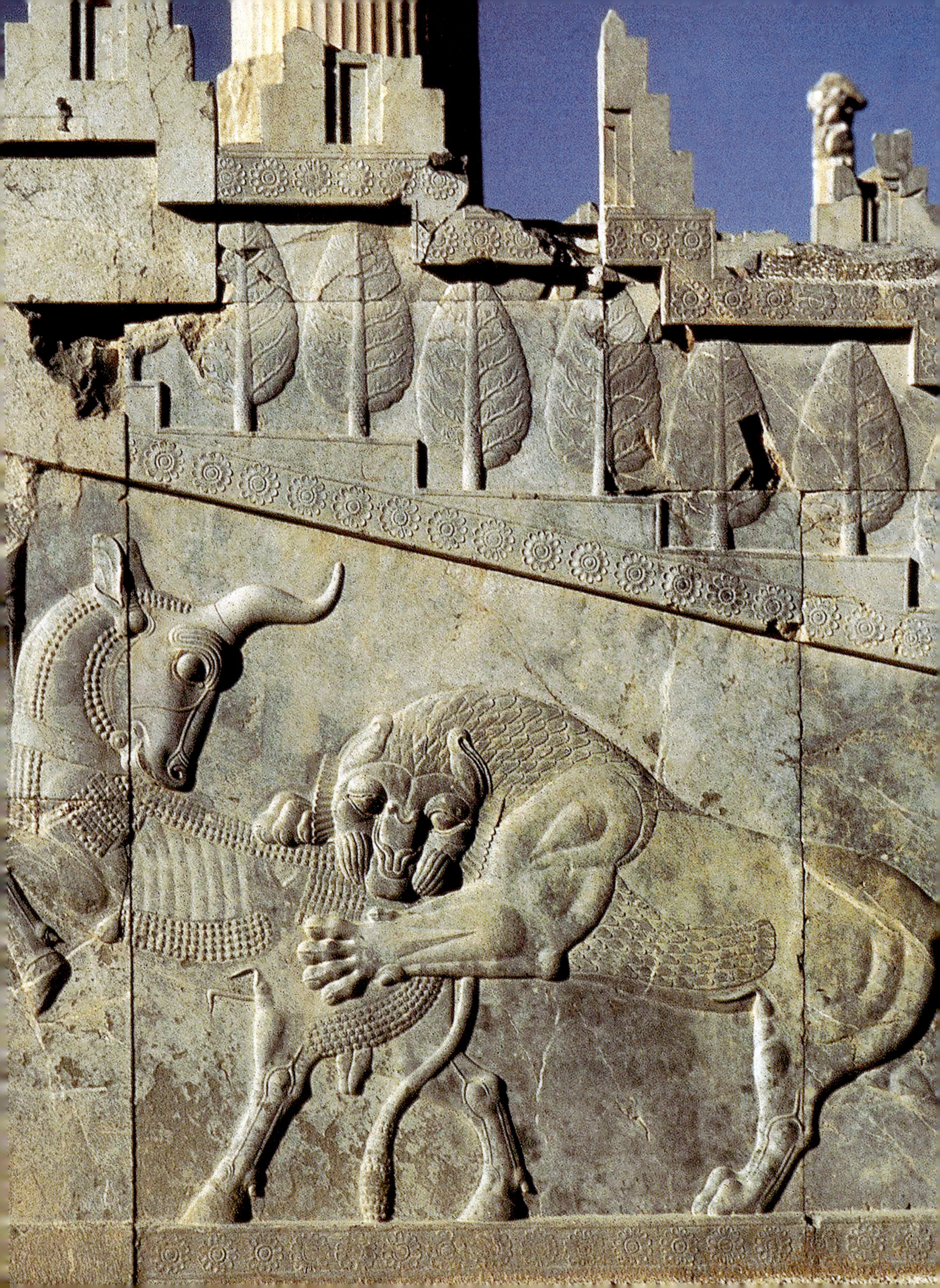

The GLORIES of PERSIA

MANY HISTORIANS BELIEVE THAT THE FIRST PERSIANS were nomads from central Asia known as the Aryans. Sometime around 1800 to 1500 BCE, groups of Aryans began to migrate southward and settle among the peoples of the Iranian plateau. By the ninth century BCE, two major Aryan tribes dominated the land. The Medes ruled over the kingdom of Media in northwestern Iran. The Persians lived mainly to the south, in a region called Fars or Parsa.

Around 550 BCE Cyrus II took the throne of Parsa. Cyrus was a brilliant military commander who led his armies to victory over Media. He went on to conquer the kingdoms of Lydia (in modern-day Turkey) and Babylonia (in today's Iraq). Persian forces also seized Greek colonies on the coast of the Aegean Sea. The empire established by Cyrus the Great was known as the Achaemenid Persian Empire, after the legendary founder of the king's dynasty, or royal family line.

Opposite: A lion and bull battle on a staircase in the palace of King Darius I at Persepolis.

Darius sits on his throne, holding two symbols of Persian royalty: a scepter and a lotus blossom.

Darius I, who became king in 522 BCE, took the Achaemenid Persian Empire to its greatest heights of power and glory. Darius extended Persian control over an area reaching as far east as the Indus River in India and as far north as the Danube River in southeastern Europe. He built a network of royal roads connecting the far-flung lands of his realm. He also built splendid palaces and other monuments at two of his capital cities, Susa and Persepolis.

About two hundred years after Darius built his vast empire, the ancient Greeks took it away. Greek forces under the command of Alexander the Great marched across Persia, defeating the armies of the last Achaemenid king. Alexander looted Susa and burned Persepolis to the ground. He conquered Babylonia, Egypt, and all the other lands of the once-great Persian Empire.

In the centuries following the Greek conquest, a series of different peoples and dynasties ruled over Persia. The Seleucid dynasty, founded by one of Alexander's generals, introduced many elements of Greek culture to the Middle East. The Parthians, an Iranian people originally from central Asia, established a prosperous empire that endured for more than three hundred years. Then, in the third century CE, the Parthians fell to a Persian dynasty called the Sassanians. The Sassanian kings founded a second Persian Empire, recapturing many of the lost lands of the old empire and reviving the glories of the past.

In 642 CE Arab Muslim armies overthrew the last Sassanian king. That conquest marked the end of the ancient Persian empires. It also introduced a new religion, Islam, which would remain a powerful influence in Iran to the present day.

A fourth-century CE silver plate shows a Sassanian king hunting deer.

> A variety of systems of dating have been used by different cultures throughout history. Many historians now prefer to use BCE (Before Common Era) and CE (Common Era) instead of BC (Before Christ) and AD (Anno Domini), out of respect for the diversity of the world's peoples.

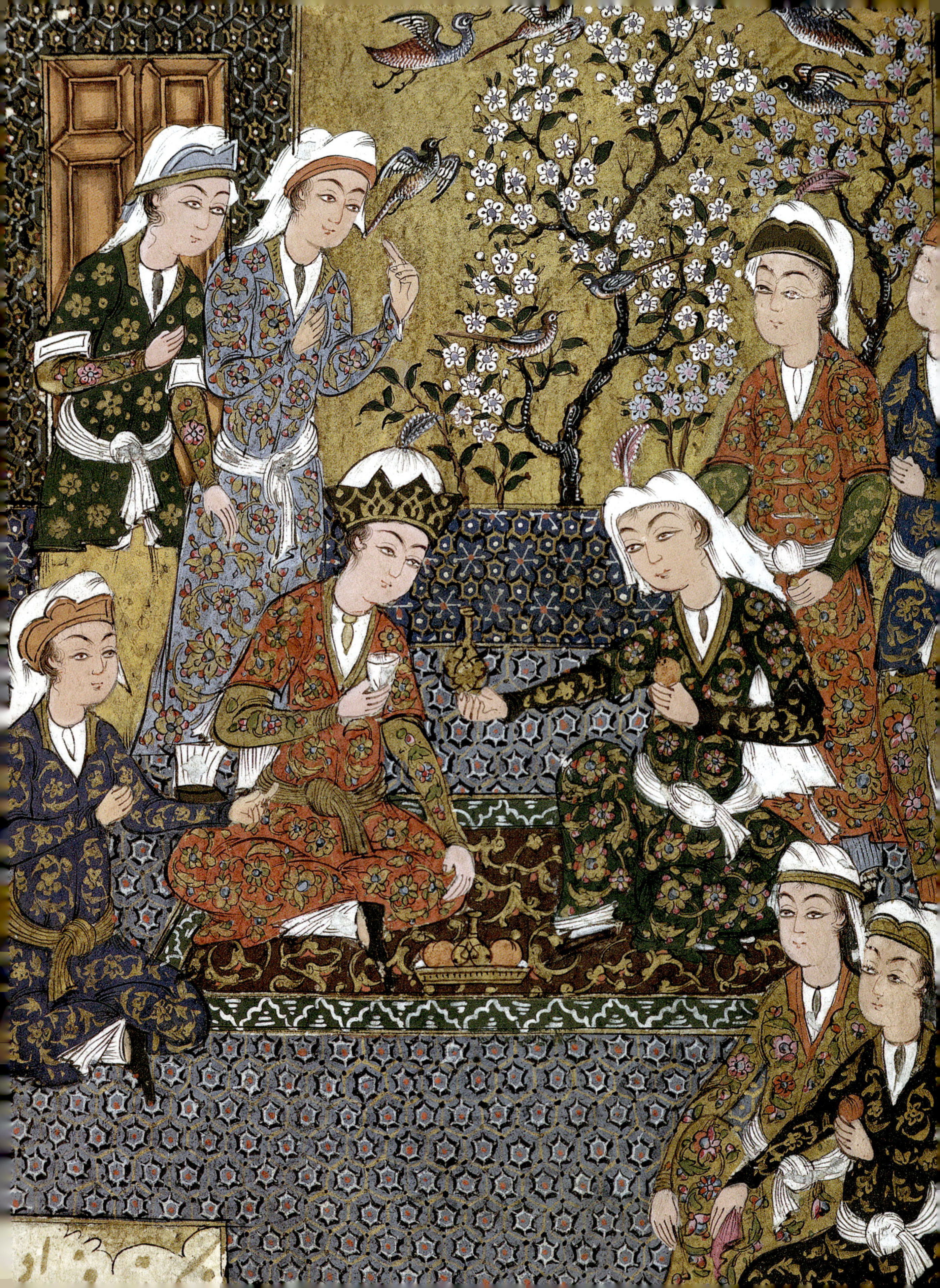

KINGS, NOBLES, *and* COMMONERS

THE KINGS OF ANCIENT PERSIA CLAIMED THAT THEIR right to rule came directly from their god, Ahura Mazda. As the god's chosen representative on earth, the king enjoyed tremendous power and majesty. He also had a sacred responsibility to live according to the divine laws, ruling in justice, compassion, and righteousness.

Persia's kings controlled their sprawling domains through a sophisticated government system. Beginning in early imperial times, the empire was divided into twenty provinces, or satrapies (SAY-truh-peez). The king appointed loyal Persian nobles to serve as the governors of each satrapy. A host of other officials performed a wide variety of roles in the provincial governments. In addition, a number of high-ranking government officials served at the royal court. These included the king's advisers, the heads of government departments, court judges, and royal scribes.

High-ranking government officials, military officers, and priests belonged to the Persian upper class. This small, powerful group also

Opposite: Persian kings lived in magnificent palaces, surrounded by every luxury.

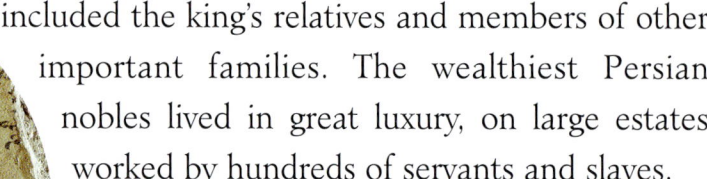

A servant carries a jug in this scene from a wall painting in a Persian palace.

included the king's relatives and members of other important families. The wealthiest Persian nobles lived in great luxury, on large estates worked by hundreds of servants and slaves.

Because most ancient Persian texts focused on the upper class, we do not know much about the lives of less privileged people. There was a small but thriving middle class. This class was made up of merchants and skilled workers such as carpenters, metalworkers, and weavers. The great majority of Persians, however, belonged to the lower class. These downtrodden people included both paid freemen and unpaid serfs. Most freemen were unskilled laborers or farmers who scraped out a living on their own small plots of land. Serfs worked in fields belonging to rich landowners. A landowner allowed a serf to live and work on a parcel of land, and in exchange the serf owed the owner a sizeable share of the harvest.

At the bottom of the social scale were the slaves. Slaves might be prisoners taken in war, freemen enslaved for debt or crime, or children born to a slave. In general, Persian slaves were well treated. In fact, slaves who belonged to well-to-do nobles often lived better than poor farmers or serfs.

From the king at the head of society to the husband at the head of the farm family, Persian society was dominated by men. Women generally were expected to dedicate themselves to their responsibilities as wives and mothers. Most women received little education and had little or no say over matters affecting their lives. These restrictions were reflected in Persian mythology. For the most part, the women of the myths lived in a male-dominated world. In this book we will meet several mythical women known almost exclusively for their roles as the mothers of powerful heroes.

The TEACHINGS of ZARATHUSTRA

THE ARYAN NOMADS WHO LIVED IN CENTRAL ASIA thousands of years ago believed in a multitude of gods, goddesses, and other supernatural beings. These deities held power over the sun, moon, sky, water, wind, fertility, war, and many other aspects of nature and everyday life. Sometimes the gods were kindly and generous. At other times they could be cruel. The people tried to win the favor of these unpredictable beings through prayers and religious rituals.

Sometime between 1800 and 1500 BCE, the prophet Zarathustra (also known as Zardosht or Zoroaster) revolutionized the ancient Aryans' beliefs. Zarathustra condemned the worship of many gods. He taught that there was only one supreme deity, Ahura Mazda. This all-good, all-wise god created the universe and all the good things in it.

Zarathustra also emphasized the importance of personal choice and responsibility. According to his teachings, Ahura Mazda is engaged in a constant battle with an evil spirit called Angra Mainyu.

That cosmic battle between good and evil is central to life on earth as well. All men and women are born with free will, meaning that they have the freedom to choose how to live their lives. Those who choose to follow the path of goodness and truth give strength to Ahura Mazda. That hastens the day when the supreme god will triumph over Angra Mainyu, and the world will be cleansed of evil and suffering.

When the ancient Persians and other Aryan tribes migrated to the Iranian plateau, they brought Zarathustra's teachings with them. As the centuries went by, the prophet's message developed into a religion known as Zoroastrianism. This new faith combined Zarathustra's ideas with elements of earlier Aryan beliefs and practices. The Achaemenid kings, especially Darius I, embraced Zoroastrianism. Eight centuries later, the Sassanians made it the official religion of their new Persian Empire.

Above: The prophet Zarathustra, founder of the Zoroastrian religion

Below: A winged symbol of Ahura Mazda hovers over the war chariot of Darius I, reflecting the idea that the king is guided by the deity.

Following the Arab conquest in the seventh century CE, most Persians converted to Islam. Today there are fewer than 200,000 followers of Zoroastrianism in the world, living mainly in Iran and India, with smaller communities in the United States, Canada, and parts of Europe. Despite its declining numbers, this ancient faith has left behind a powerful legacy. Scholars believe that the principles of Zoroastrianism—including ideas about a supreme god, heaven and hell, and a final judgment day—influenced the development of major world religions including Judaism, Christianity, Islam, and Buddhism.

The SACRED FIRE

THE RELIGION THAT DEVELOPED FROM ZARATHUSTRA'S teachings combined the prophet's revolutionary ideas with rites and practices reaching back countless years. The main instrument of Zoroastrian worship was fire. The early Aryans had worshipped their gods with burnt offerings. For the followers of Zoroastrianism, fire became a symbol of truth and purity, marking a path to the great Ahura Mazda himself.

Many Zoroastrian religious rituals were (and still are) conducted in the presence of a sacred fire. At first, these fires were built outdoors or in household hearths. Later, the Persians began to build special fire temples. Priests tended the flames that burned on altars in these magnificent stone buildings.

Another important feature of Zoroastrian worship dating back to earlier traditions was the *haoma* ritual. *Haoma* was the name of an ancient god of immortality as well as a plant. The juice of the plant was

Elegant courtiers enjoy the Zoroastrian feast of Sada, celebrating the discovery of fire.

a mild stimulant. Priests drank *haoma* juice as part of their chief worship ceremony, the *yasna*, in order to become more open to divine visions.

The priests of ancient Persia were called magi. These honored men presided over a daily round of temple rituals, reciting many complicated prayers, hymns, and sacred formulas by heart. Zoroastrians believed that the correct performance of these rituals honored Ahura Mazda and also helped the god in his battle against evil.

Ordinary Persians worshipped not only at the fire temples but also at home and outdoors. They might stand beside a river or face the sun, offering their prayers to the great god who created the waters and the heavenly bodies. Zarathustra is said to have directed his followers to pray five times a day.

The prophet also prescribed seven great religious festivals. On these holy days, the entire community came together to worship Ahura Mazda and share a joyous feast. The highest holiday was the New Year festival, or Nav Roz, held on the first day of spring. Today Zoroastrians still observe this ancient festival, celebrating the renewal of life and the glorious day to come when good will triumph over evil once and for all.

A worshipper carries a *barsom*, a bundle of sacred sticks used in religious ceremonies.

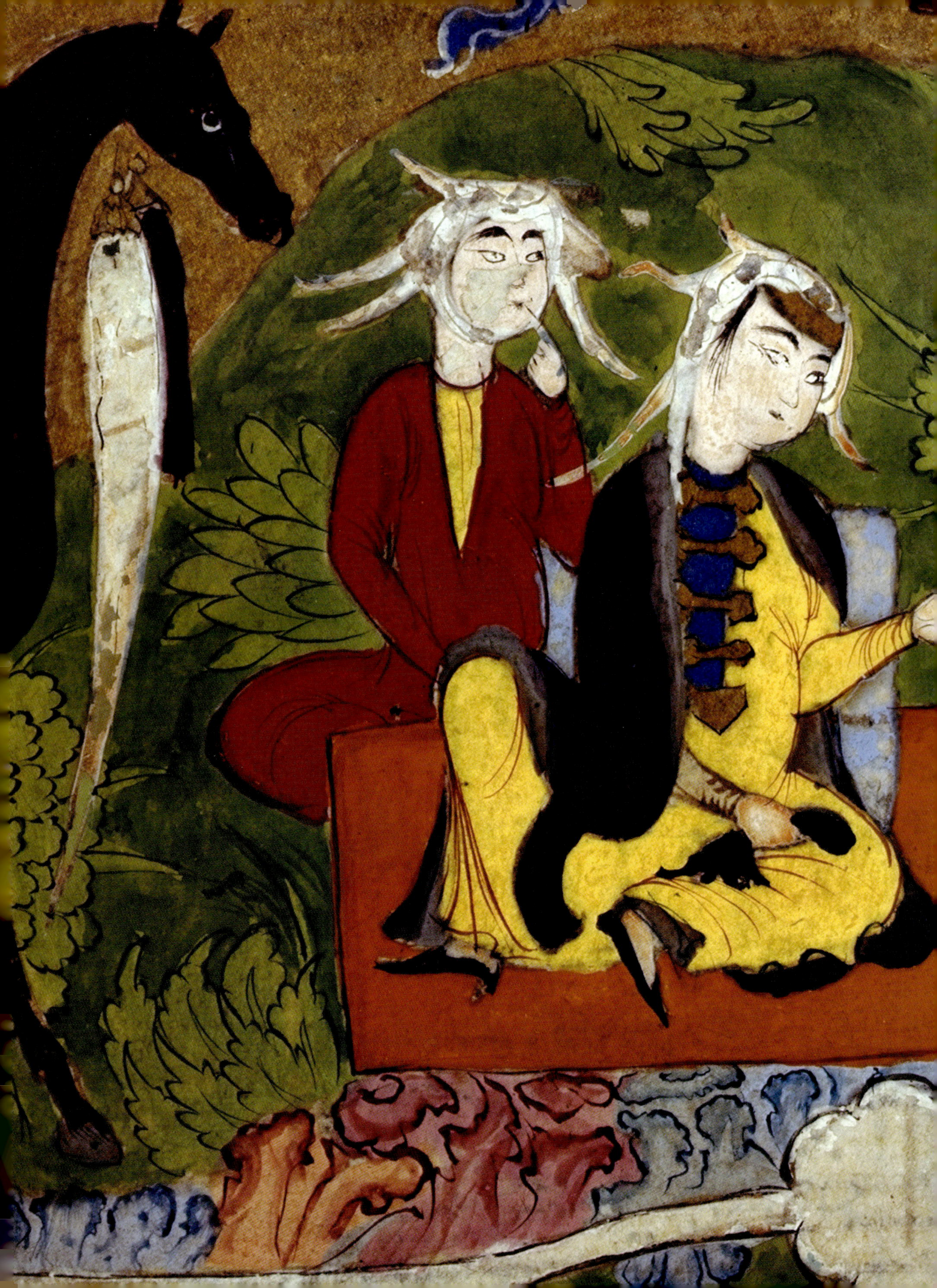

Part 2
TIMELESS TALES of ANCIENT PERSIA

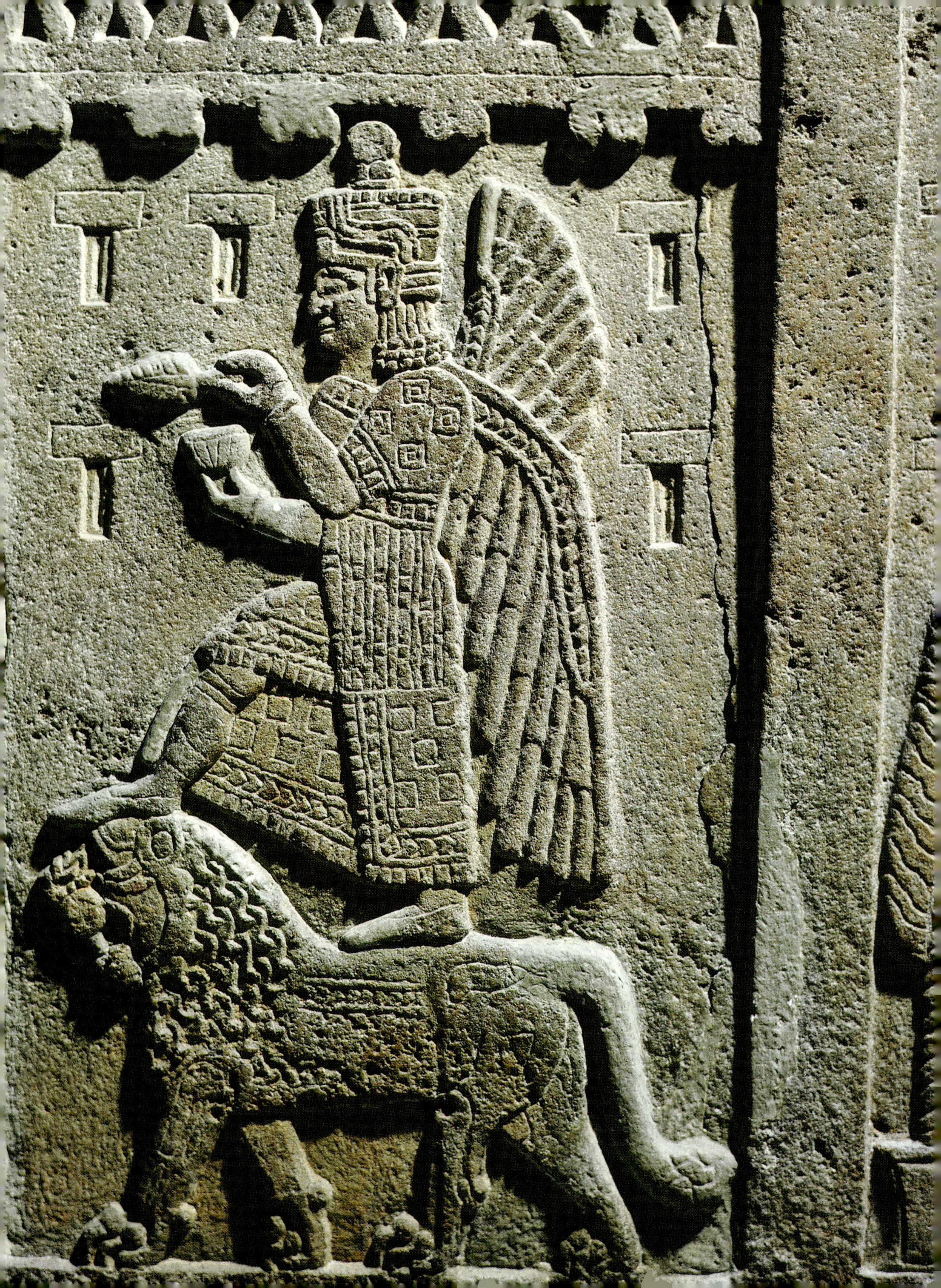

THE ORIGINS *of the* WORLD *and* HUMANS

Ahura Mazda and the Good Creation

THE EARLY PERSIANS TOLD SEVERAL DIFFERENT STORIES about the origins of the world and the first people. Their best-known creation story has come down to us through the teachings of Zarathustra. As the founder of Zoroastrianism, Zarathustra often retold the ancient myths of his people, drawing on the lessons in the stories to reinforce his message.

The Zoroastrian creation story revolves around Ahura Mazda, the supreme god who is the source of all that is good in the universe. Ahura Mazda watches over the world with the help of an army of heavenly beings. These divinities include a group of powerful angels called the Amesha Spentas ("Holy Immortals"), a host of divine spirits called the *yazatas* ("spirits worthy of worship"), and the *fravashis*, which are the immortal souls of mortal men and women.

Opposing Ahura Mazda is Angra Mainyu. This devil-like spirit is the source of all that is evil. He constantly strives to destroy the Good

Opposite: Perched atop a fierce lion, Ahura Mazda presents the gift of holy water.

Previous page: A painting inspired by a twelfth-century Persian poem shows a princess conversing with a lovelorn stonemason.

Creation of Ahura Mazda and to lure people into his world of lies and wickedness. A host of horrible demons assist him in his wicked schemes.

According to Zoroastrian beliefs, the constant struggle between good and evil led to the creation. Ahura Mazda made the world for a specific purpose: to serve as the arena in which he would confront his eternal enemy. His first battle with Angra Mainyu gave the world its present form and set the heavenly bodies in motion. At one point, it looked as if the evil spirit would triumph, resulting in the destruction of all life on earth. In the end, though, Ahura Mazda and his angels proved more powerful.

CAST *of* CHARACTERS

Ahura Mazda (ah-HOOR-uh MAZ-duh) Supreme god; also known as Ohrmazd or God
Angra Mainyu (ANG-ruh MUN-yoo) Spirit of darkness and evil; also known as Ahriman
Gayo-maretan (gah-YOH-mah-re-tun) First human
Mashye (mash-YUH) and **Mashyane** (mash-YUH-nuh) Father and mother of the human race

The Light and the Darkness

BEFORE THE WORLD was created, Ahura Mazda lived above in a kingdom of endless light. Far below, in an abyss of eternal darkness, dwelt the evil spirit Angra Mainyu. Between the two was a vast empty space, so that good and evil existed without contact.

Angra Mainyu was so ignorant that he was not aware of Ahura Mazda's existence. But the supreme lord knew all about the wicked spirit. In his wisdom he understood that he had to create a place to confront and defeat evil.

So Ahura Mazda set the Good Creation in motion. He began by forming a substance of pure spirit. The bright white spirit filled the universe with radiance. When its light pierced the darkness, Angra Mainyu rushed out to destroy it. But the glory of the spirit was too great to overcome. Defeated, the evil one slunk back to his gloomy kingdom. There he produced many terrible fiends and demons, whose sole purpose for existence was destruction.

Ahura Mazda already knew how the conflict between good and evil would end. Even so, in his infinite goodness and mercy, he went to speak with Angra Mainyu. "Save yourself and your creatures," said the wise lord. "Offer praise to the light, and I will grant you immortality."

Angra Mainyu just laughed at the god's generous offer. He believed that the supreme lord must be weak and frightened to come begging for peace. "I will never praise you!" he shouted. "I will destroy you forever and force all your creatures to worship me instead!"

Now, Ahura Mazda knew that the evil one could not really defeat him. But he also could see far into the future, to

> **NINETY DAYS AND NIGHTS THE HEAVENLY ANGELS WERE CONTENDING . . . WITH THE . . . DEMONS OF THE EVIL SPIRIT.**
>
> —THE *BUNDAHISHN*

This ancient Roman statue may depict Angra Mainyu as a snake attacking Ahura Mazda and his Good Creation.

Ahura Mazda and the Good Creation | 33

the days of humankind. Among men and women, there would be many misguided individuals who would practice wrong more than right. If the conflict between good and evil went on too long, Angra Mainyu might be able to persuade those people to join his side. So Ahura Mazda proposed that the war last for a fixed period of time only. For nine thousand years, the two enemies would fight, and then their contest would be over.

Angra Mainyu foolishly agreed to the time limit. The moment he gave his consent, his doom was sealed. Reciting a powerful prayer, Ahura Mazda unveiled a vision of the future. When Angra Mainyu beheld his own utter downfall, he shrieked in horror and fell back into his gloomy pit. There he would remain for three thousand years, stunned and powerless.

The First Battle

While Angra Mainyu lay helpless, Ahura Mazda was preparing for battle. First the wise lord shaped the spirit of light into a host of divinities. He made the six Amesha Spentas, whose names are Good Thought, Best Order, Desirable Dominion, Holy Devotion, Wholeness, and Immortality. He created the *yazatas*, divine spirits who would aid in the battle against evil. Ahura Mazda also made the immortal souls of men and women, known as the *fravashis*.

Next Ahura Mazda created the world in the shape of a giant sphere. The top half formed a dome, and the bottom half was filled with sweet waters. He lighted the sky with the sun, moon, and stars. He made the flat disk of the earth and set it floating on the waters.

In the center of the earth, Ahura Mazda placed a sturdy tree, a white ox, and a human called Gayo-maretan. All of the god's creations were

The coming of the evil spirit knocked some of the stars from the heavens.

perfect. The tree was smooth, without bark or thorn. The skin of the ox was as bright as the moon, and the human's body shined like the sun.

By now, three thousand years had passed. Angra Mainyu finally revived from his stupor. At the sight of the Good Creation, the evil spirit was filled with rage and envy. With a monstrous cry, he summoned his demons and sprang forth to attack the world.

The whole of creation shook with the coming of evil. The sky shattered, dislodging the sun, moon, and stars from their fixed stations. The heavenly bodies began to move across the sky. The sun brought the first day and night, and the moon commenced the marking of the months.

Angra Mainyu surged on through the sweet waters, fouling them with salt. Then, like a serpent striking its prey, he pierced the earth in the middle. The force of the blow sent ripples across the land, forming

Ahura Mazda and the Good Creation

Angra Mainyu created all the evil things of the world, including the poisonous snakes and spiders.

the high mountains and deep valleys. The evil one unleashed the whirlwinds and sandstorms. He poisoned the great tree and all the plants. He set loose venomous snakes, lizards, and scorpions, until the whole earth was covered with noxious creatures. The world was so black and injured at midday that it seemed like the darkest of nights.

Last of all Angra Mainyu turned his wrath on the white ox and the mortal, Gayo-maretan. He attacked them with many moral and physical evils: greed, lust, laziness, pain, hunger, disease. The ox's body shattered into pieces. The human lived on in the blighted landscape. While he struggled to survive, the heavenly angels battled the demons, each good spirit grappling with its evil counterpart. After thirty years Gayo-maretan finally fell to the demon of death.

The Triumph of the Light

"My victory is complete!" cried Angra Mainyu. "The Good Creation is ruined!"

The evil spirit turned to lead his forces home in triumph. Suddenly, a shining angel clad in the golden armor of a warrior blocked his path.

Behind the angel was arrayed a mighty host of *fravashis*, mounted on warhorses, spears in hand. "Now that you have come into the world, we will not let you go," said the heavenly forces.

Angra Mainyu cried out in rage, but it was too late. In a flash Ahura Mazda surrounded the sky with a thick wall. The world that the supreme lord had created became his enemy's prison. To this day the souls of the righteous stand guard over that fortress, preventing the evil one from escaping.

Once Angra Mainyu was trapped, Ahura Mazda and his angels set to work reviving the world. They crushed the fallen tree and mixed its juices with water. The mixture rained down upon the earth, washing away all the noxious creatures. The seas and lakes formed, and the rivers began to flow.

The parts of the ox's body still lay scattered across the land. As the rains fell, all kinds of plants began to spring from the animal's organs. The seed that the ox had spilled when he died rose up to the moon. Purified by the light, it returned to the earth and gave life to many different species of animals.

Gayo-maretan's body had also given forth seed at his death. That seed was carried up into the sky and purified in the radiant light of the sun. It returned to the earth, where it lay buried for forty years, warmed by the sun and nourished by the life-giving rains.

Finally, the first human couple, Mashye and Mashyane, grew up out of the soil. From this couple would come all the generations of men and women. Thus humankind, like all the rest of the Good Creation, arose from the first battle between good and evil.

THE EARLY PERSIANS SPEAK
The FIRST SIN

According to a twelfth-century Persian text called the *Bundahishn*, or "Book of Original Creation," the seed of Gayo-maretan gave rise to the first human couple, Mashye and Mashyane. Although Ahura Mazda told the pair to devote themselves to goodness, Angra Mainyu lured them away from the right path. Under his influence Mashye and Mashyane committed the first sin, naming the evil spirit as the creator.

Above: In this Persian painting, Angra Mainyu tempts Mashye and Mashyane into eating a forbidden fruit.

As a result of their wicked lie, evil and violence entered the world. The corruption reached its climax when the new parents devoured their first children. Ahura Mazda had to do away with Mashye and Mashyane's appetite for their offspring before the couple could fulfill their destiny, giving birth to the ancestors of the human race.

> Aûharmazd* spoke to [Mashye and Mashyane] thus: "You are man[kind], you are the ancestry of the world, and you are created perfect in devotion by me; perform devotedly the duty of the law, think good thoughts, speak good words, do good deeds, and worship no demons!" . . . The first words spoken by [the couple] were these, that Aûharmazd created the water and earth, plants and animals, the stars, moon, and sun, and all prosperity. . . . And, afterwards, antagonism [hostility] rushed into their minds, and their minds were thoroughly corrupted, and they exclaimed that the evil spirit created the water and earth, plants and animals, and the other things as aforesaid. That false speech was spoken through the will of the demons, and the evil spirit possessed himself of this first enjoyment from them; through that false speech they both became wicked. . . .
>
> From them was born in nine months a pair, male and female; and owing to tenderness [appetite] for offspring the mother devoured one, and the father one. And, afterwards, Aûharmazd took tenderness for offspring away from them, so that one may nourish a child, and the child may remain. And from them arose seven pairs, male and female . . . and from them the constant continuance of the generations of the world arose.

*Aûharmazd is a later version of the name Ahura Mazda.

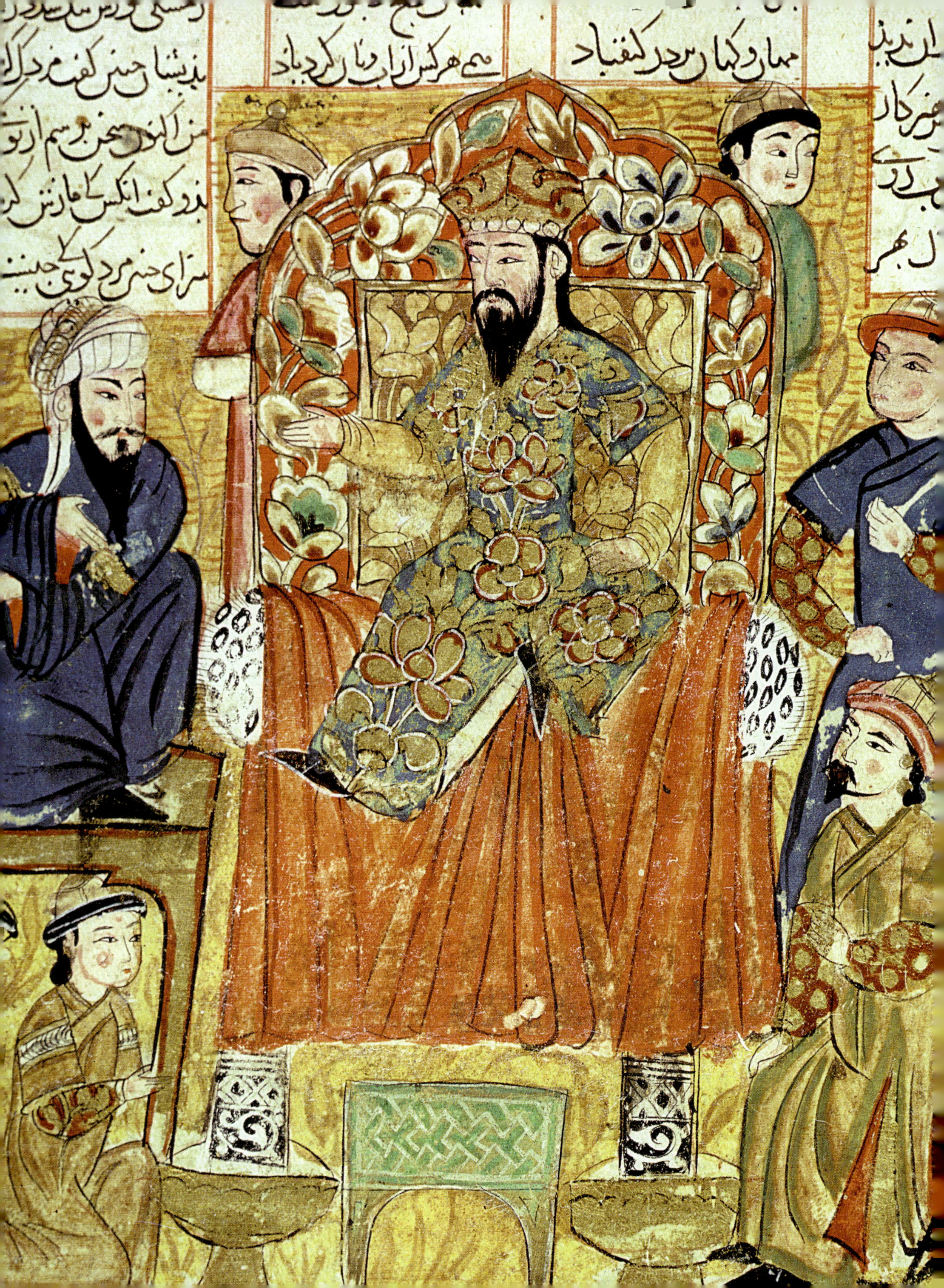

TALES FROM *the* SHAHNAMEH

The First Earthly Kings

PERSIAN MYTHOLOGY WAS CONCERNED NOT ONLY WITH the cosmic battle between good and evil but also with the grand adventures of kings and heroes. Over time Persian priests and scribes wove together the ancient heroic tales of their people to create a fabulous history of the empire. The kings in this mythical history had nearly godlike powers. They introduced civilization at the very beginnings of the world. They also defended the emerging culture of Persia from monsters, demons, and other evil forces.

The best-known source of Persian heroic tales is the *Shahnameh*, or "Book of Kings," written by the poet Ferdowsi in the late tenth to early eleventh centuries CE. Ferdowsi based his famous epic poem on ancient Iranian myths and Zoroastrian traditions. The *Shahnameh* tells the story of Persia and its kings all the way from the creation of the world to the Arab conquest. It celebrates the glorious cultural heritage of the Persian people. It also traces the Zoroastrian religion from its dawn to the defeat of the last Zoroastrian king.

Opposite: According to mythology, the first Persian kings were superhuman beings who ruled over the entire world.

The opening chapters of Ferdowsi's book are based on ancient myths about the early days of the world. According to the *Shahnameh*, the first human, Kayumars,* was also the first king. Kayumars gave the world law, religion, and other important elements of culture. He was succeeded on the throne by his grandson, Hushang. This wise king introduced irrigation and discovered the secret of making fire.

Persia's next mythical ruler was Tahmures, known as the Binder of Demons. One of this king's most celebrated acts was his capture of Ahriman. In our first myth, we saw that the supreme god Ahura Mazda trapped the evil spirit after their first battle. Ahriman could not completely destroy the world from within his prison, but he was still capable of spreading lies, wickedness, and misfortune. Tahmures temporarily put a halt to these dark deeds, in a way that was particularly humiliating to the evil spirit.

CAST *of* CHARACTERS

Kayumars (ka-yoo-MARS) First king of Persia; also known as Gayo-maretan

Siamak (shih-ah-MAK) Son of Kayumars

Ahriman (AH-rih-mun) Spirit of darkness and evil; also known as Angra Mainyu

Sorush (sow-ROOSH) An angel of God

Ohrmazd (OR-muzd) The supreme god; also known as Ahura Mazda or God

Hushang (hoo-SHANG) Grandson of Kayumars; a Persian king

Tahmures (ta-MOOR-us) Son of Hushang; a Persian king

---

*The *Shahnameh* was written in a late form of the Persian language called New Persian or Farsi. In that language, Gayo-maretan (the world's first human in our earlier myth) is known as Kayumars, the supreme god Ahura Mazda is called Ohrmazd, and the evil spirit Angra Mainyu is called Ahriman.

The Sorrow of Kayumars

WHO WAS THE first man to sit upon the throne of Persia? Ancient tales tell us that it was Kayumars. When the world was young, this good king lived in the mountains. He dressed himself and his people in animal skins. It was Kayumars who gave us the arts of preparing food and clothing in those early days when civilization was still in its infancy.

Kayumars also introduced the first code of laws. People came from all over the world to receive his laws and hear his wise counsel. Even the animals, both wild and tame, came to honor him. Seated on his high throne, Kayumars shined like the sun in his goodness and glory. All who saw him knelt down as though in prayer, awed by his God-given splendor. Thus began the very idea of reverence, which would give rise to religion.

Kayumars and his queen were blessed with a son named Siamak. This handsome youth was wise, skillful, and eager for fame. The sight of him filled the king's heart with happiness. One thing only did Kayumars fear: the thought of somehow losing his beloved child.

For thirty years Kayumars reigned in peace. But even his royal

Kayumars's gifts to the world included the first clothing, made from leopard skins.

virtues could not hold back evil forever. Ahriman was growing more and more jealous of the king's glory. Finally, the evil spirit could stand it no longer. He summoned his own son, a dark demon who was as fearless and savage as a wolf. At his father's command, the mighty demon gathered an army and set out to seize the throne.

That night the blessed angel Sorush, who watches over the children of Ohrmazd, appeared before Prince Siamak. The young man seethed with fury when the angel told him about the plot against his father. Quickly Siamak assembled his own warriors. He arrayed himself in a leopard skin, for armor had not yet been invented. Then he strode forth at the head of his troops to stop the demon army.

The two forces met on a broad, dusty plain. Siamak stepped forward to challenge the son of Ahriman. The young prince used all his strength in the deadly hand-to-hand combat, but the dark demon proved too powerful. He sank his deadly claws into the prince's unprotected body, and the noble son of the king perished.

When Kayumars heard of his son's death, the world turned black around him. Falling from his throne, he wailed in anguish and tore his face until his cheeks ran with blood. For an entire year, the king wept without ceasing, and the entire kingdom mourned with him.

At last Ohrmazd sent Sorush with a message for the king: "Weep no more. It is time to collect your troops and rid the earth of that vile demon."

When he heard the angel's words, Kayumars wiped away his tears. Lifting his face to the heavens, he asked Ohrmazd for strength against his enemies. Then the king turned his heart and mind to vengeance.

Prince Siamak had left behind a son named Hushang. This splendid youth was the very image of his father. As soon as Kayumars resolved on war, he sent for his beloved grandson. "I mean to march

THE ... DEMON SUNK HIS CLAWS INTO THE PRINCE'S UNPROTECTED BODY AND STRETCHED THE NOBLE SIAMAK IN THE DUST.

—THE *SHAHNAMEH*

against the dark demon," said the king. "But I am old and worn out. You must command my army."

Hushang leaped at the chance to avenge his father's death. Soon the royal army was on the march, with the king's intrepid young grandson leading. The ranks of the army were filled out with warrior angels, as well as leopards, lions, wolves, tigers, and other fierce creatures.

The dark demon himself led the enemy forces. But the evil host could not withstand the fury of the king's army. The angels and roaring beasts utterly destroyed the demon warriors. Meanwhile, Hushang

The First Earthly Kings | 45

battled his father's murderer. The prince seized the son of Ahriman like a lion gripping its prey. He tore the dark demon's body in two. Then he cut off the monster's head and trampled it in the mud.

At last Kayumars had achieved his vengeance. With a peaceful sigh, the good king lay down and died. The world was deprived of his glory, but his might and wisdom would never be forgotten.

Hushang and the Gift of Fire

After the death of Kayumars, Hushang ascended the throne. Like his grandfather, the new king was wise and good. His reign saw the establishment of justice and law all across the land.

Hushang also introduced many valuable arts to the untamed world. Chief among these was the secret of making fire. One day the king was riding in the mountains when a monster suddenly appeared. The beast was huge and black, with eyes like raging pools of blood. Smoke billowed from its gaping jaws, plunging the world into darkness. As the monster rushed toward him, Hushang calmly picked up a stone and hurled it with all his might. The monster fled, and the stone collided with a large boulder, producing a spark. Curious, the king hit the boulder again. Again came the flash, as the ironstone struck the flint rock. Thus Hushang discovered the fiery nature of flint, which gives off sparks whenever one strikes it with iron.

Bowing low, the king thanked Ohrmazd for the gift of fire. That night he and his companions built a towering bonfire and celebrated with a great feast. From that day forth, faithful men and women have offered their prayers toward the sacred fire.

Hushang also found many earthly uses for the heaven-sent flames. He taught his people how to use fire to separate iron from the rocks.

Hushang taught the people how to irrigate their fields with water drawn from the rivers.

He invented the forge, so that blacksmiths could make axes, saws, hatchets, and other tools and weapons from iron. With the help of their new tools, farmers planted and harvested the first crops. The king showed them how to dig irrigation canals, so that the rivers and lakes would water their fields.

Hushang also used his God-given authority to separate the animals. Some beasts remained wild for hunting. Others were tamed and set to work for humankind. Oxen and donkeys began to pull plows and haul loads. Cows, sheep, and goats provided their meat, milk, and hides.

For forty years the heavens revolved over the throne of Hushang. The king toiled without ceasing, and the earth flourished under his care. Then he departed for a better life in heaven, leaving behind his good name and the fruits of his labor.

The First Earthly Kings

By the time Tahmures took the throne, farmers had learned how to cultivate the earth and plant crops.

The Binder of Demons

The next man to sit on the throne of Persia was Hushang's son, Tahmures. This wise and noble ruler continued his father's good works. He taught the farmers how to shear the sheep and goats, spin the wool, and weave garments and carpets. He trained the wild hawks and falcons to assist the hunters. He told his people to praise the creator, who had given them dominion over the animals.

The greatest achievement of Tahmures was his victory over the demons. When the king took the throne, he swore to cleanse the world of evil and ignorance. Shining with the light of his God-given glory, he went forth to battle the evil spirit. With his powerful magic spells, he transformed Ahriman into the shape of a horse. He placed a bridle over the evil one's head and a saddle on his back. For thirty years the triumphant king rode around the earth on the back of his conquered enemy.

When the demons beheld their leader's humiliation, they roared in outrage. Banding together in a great army, they prepared to overthrow Tahmures. But the king soon learned of their plans and led his warriors forth to battle.

> **THE KING BOUND AHRIMAN BY SPELLS AND SAT ON HIM, USING HIM AS A MOUNT TO TOUR THE WORLD.**
> —THE *SHAHNAMEH*

The army of the demons was like a vast tide of gloom. Their breath blackened the air, and their foul stench rose to the heavens. Then Tahmures strode forth at the head of his forces. The king quickly subdued two-thirds of the demons with his spells and disposed of the other third with his massive iron mace.

Bound and wounded, the remaining demons groveled in the dust. "Do not destroy us," they begged. "We can teach you a valuable new art."

So Tahmures agreed to spare the lives of the demons. He freed them from their chains and released Ahriman from his enchantment. The conquered demons brought forth pens and ink and taught the king the art of writing. They showed him not just one script but almost thirty, including the Persian, Chinese, Arab, and Western ways of writing. Thus from the servants of the evil spirit came a great blessing for humankind.

For thirty more years, Tahmures ruled in wisdom and righteousness. Then his days, too, came to an end. Though he passed away, the world will always remember the noble king honored as the Binder of Demons.

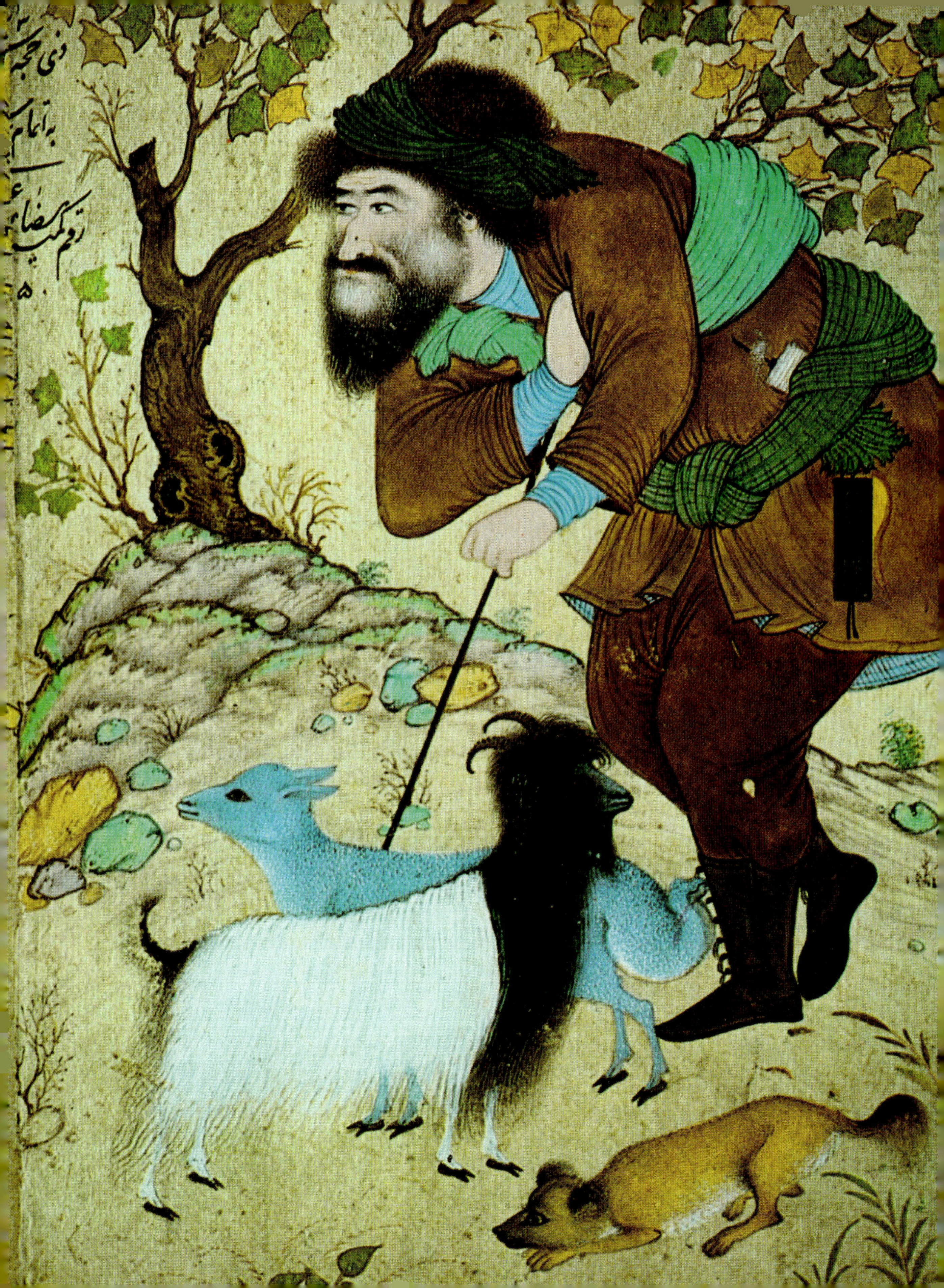
ذی حجه
به اتمام
رقم کمینه رضا

The GOLDEN AGE

Yima Saves the World

"THE SORROW OF KAYUMARS" ON PAGE 43 TOLD US THAT Kayumars was the world's first mortal king. That story was based on the *Shahnameh*. In a number of other Persian tales, the role of first king went to Yima. Often called the greatest of all kings, Yima presided over a golden age of peace and abundance. In fact, the world was such a paradise under his reign that the king had to enlarge it three times to make room for all the people and animals.

The golden age of Yima came to an end with a worldwide disaster. The story of that catastrophe is similar to tales of a "great flood" told by ancient peoples all over the world. In the ancient Persian myth, deadly cold replaces the floodwaters. After the creator god Ahura Mazda warns Yima that a terrible winter is coming, the king builds a giant *vara*, or enclosure. He fills this safe haven with the best of all the plants, animals, and people on earth. When the killing storms strike, the seeds of new life live on inside Yima's *vara*.

Opposite: The humble shepherd Yima became the greatest of all Persian kings.

Our retelling of the myth of Yima is drawn from the Avesta. This collection of ancient prayers, hymns, and other sacred texts is the holiest book of the Zoroastrian religion. The central part of the Avesta is believed to contain the words of the prophet Zarathustra himself. Zarathustra denounced Yima as a sinner who worshipped the ancient gods with animal sacrifices. As a result of the prophet's condemnation, a wide variety of contradictory tales developed about the mythical ruler. In most Persian myths, Yima still shines as the king of the golden age and the savior of life on earth. In other stories, however, he is a tragic figure who loses his throne when he dares to proclaim himself equal to Ahura Mazda.

CAST *of* CHARACTERS

Yima (YEE-mah) King of the golden age; also known as Jamshid

Ahura Mazda (ah-HOOR-uh MAZ-duh) Supreme god; also known as Ohrmazd or God

Spenta Armaiti (spen-TAH arm-ah-IH-tee) Spirit of serenity and the earth

Angra Mainyu (ANG-ruh MUN-yoo) Spirit of darkness and evil; also known as Ahriman

Years of Peace and Plenty

AT THE DAWN OF the world, there lived a good shepherd named Yima. Ahura Mazda spoke to the shepherd: "Shining Yima, will you watch over my creation and make it thrive?"

"Yes!" the shepherd answered. "I will rule over your world and nourish it! While I am king, there will be neither freezing wind nor scorching heat, neither disease nor death."

So Ahura Mazda gave Yima a golden ring and dagger. With these two symbols of his authority, the shepherd-king began his brilliant reign. For three hundred years, the world thrived under his care. There were no bitter-cold winters or blazing hot summers. There was no hunger or thirst, no sickness or old age or death. No demon dared to show his face in a world where everything was good.

Then Ahura Mazda spoke to Yima again: "Shining Yima, the earth is so prosperous that it has become overcrowded. Soon there will be no more room for the flocks of birds and the herds of animals, for the men and women and their sacred fires."

The king thanked the creator for his warning. He pressed his golden ring against the earth and thrust his golden dagger into the soil. He called out to the shining spirit of the earth: "O Spenta Armaiti, kindly open and stretch yourself afar."

There was a shudder. A groan. An ear-splitting crack. Suddenly the surface of the earth began to stretch. The horizons on all sides faded into the distance as the world grew one-third larger than it had been before.

Above: Ahura Mazda gave Yima a golden dagger as a sign of his royal power.

Left: Yima called on the angel Spenta Armaiti, whose name means "Holy Devotion."

Yima Saves the World | 53

Now came another three hundred years of peace and plenty. The population of the earth continued to multiply under the care of Yima. Again Ahura Mazda warned the king that the world was becoming too full. Again Yima pressed his ring to the ground and pierced the soil with his dagger. The earth stretched out once more, until it was two-thirds larger than it had been at the creation.

Yet another three hundred years passed. Now there were more flocks and herds and people than ever before. A third time Yima called on the shining angel Spenta Armaiti. A third time the earth grew, making room for all its creatures. And that is how the world grew twice as large as it had been at the creation. That is how it became the size it is today, thanks to good king Yima.

Three Fatal Winters

For nine hundred years, Yima had ruled over the world. Under his reign all living things had thrived. Angra Mainyu, lord of evil, could not stand the sight of such peace and abundance. Finally, the wicked spirit decided to put an end to the world's happiness.

Ahura Mazda was well aware of Angra Mainyu's evil plans. The creator spoke to the king, saying: "Shining Yima, a catastrophe is about to befall the world. Three terrible winters are coming, bringing deep snows and fierce, foul frost. All the creatures of the earth shall perish: those that live in the wilderness, those that live in the mountains, and those that live in the shelter of the valleys.

"To save the earth, you must build a *vara*. This enclosure shall be a great square, as long as a riding-ground on every side. You shall fill the *vara* with the seeds of every different plant and tree. You shall bring every kind of creature: men and women, sheep and oxen, dogs and birds. Take care that you choose only the best and most beautiful creatures, the strongest and most sweet-smelling plants. Nothing must be tainted with weakness, meanness, or deceit. Nothing must bear the evil mark of Angra Mainyu."

Yima listened carefully and followed the god's instructions. He stamped his heel on the ground and gathered up a handful of crushed earth. He kneaded the earth in his hands the way a potter kneads clay. Then he used the magical soil to build a giant *vara*, two miles long on every side. He diverted a stream so that its waters flowed through the enclosure. He raised hills, carved out valleys, and shaped every other kind of landscape. At the heart of the compound, he built a small city, with nine streets lined with pleasant houses.

Next the king planted seeds inside his *vara*. The seeds sprang up into wonderful plants and trees that would bear a never-ending supply of food. Yima settled birds along the lush banks of the stream. He found homes for all the different animals, each in its familiar surroundings. He brought hundreds of men, women, and children to the streets of the

> **[YIMA] BROUGHT THE SEEDS OF EVERY KIND OF FRUIT, THE FULLEST OF FOOD AND SWEETEST OF ODOR.**
> —THE *VENDIDAD*

Yima Saves the World | 55

A deep snow blanketed the world outside Yima's *vara*.

miniature city. Finally, when his work was finished, the king used his sacred golden ring to seal up the whole enclosure.

The sun had been shining as Yima worked on the *vara*. The moment he completed his task, the first evil winter fell. Outside the enclosure a chill breeze began to blow. A deadly frost crept over the fields and tree branches. Soon the snow lay so deep that even the tallest man could not forge a path through it. All the people, birds, and animals perished from cold and hunger.

Meanwhile, inside the *vara*, all was light and warmth. For three winters the people of this little world lived in perfect happiness. There was no lying, no envy, no poverty, decay, or disease—none of the marks with which the lord of evil stamps the bodies of mortals.

At last Angra Mainyu grew weary. The terrible storms afflicting the world faded, and the snows melted. Yima opened the door of the *vara*, and new life poured forth into the barren landscape. The earth grew a fresh green carpet of grass, shrubs, and trees. The herds grazed in the fields. The wild animals roamed the young forests. The people began to till the soil and rebuild the cities and villages. They rekindled their sacred fires and gave thanks to Ahura Mazda. And they all sang the praises of Yima, the shepherd-king who had built the *vara* and saved the world's living creatures.

THE EARLY PERSIANS SPEAK
The FALL of YIMA

Ancient Persian texts tell us that every rightful king had a quality known as *farr*, or "divine glory." This shining quality, which gave the ruler his exalted powers and authority, was a gift from Ahura Mazda. The supreme god could withdraw the divine glory from any king who strayed from the path of righteousness. According to some accounts, that dreadful fate befell the great Yima. The following passage from an ancient Zoroastrian prayer hints at the sin that brought about Yima's downfall. The king began to "delight in words of falsehood," probably by claiming that he was as great as Ahura Mazda. In punishment, the god made the *farr* fly from the foolish man's body. Soon after that, Yima was killed and a new king took the throne of Persia.

> We sacrifice unto the awful kingly Glory, made by [Ahura] Mazda. . . .
> That clave [stuck] unto the bright Yima, the good shepherd, for a long time,
>   while he ruled over the . . . earth. . . .
> He who took from the Daevas [demons] both riches and welfare, both fatness
>   and flocks, both weal [well-being] and Glory;
> In whose reign both aliments [foods] were never failing for feeding creatures,
>   flocks and men were undying, waters and plants were undrying;
> In whose reign there was neither cold wind nor hot wind, neither old age nor
>   death, nor envy made by the Daevas, in the times before his lie, before he
>   began to have delight in words of falsehood and untruth.
> But when he began to find delight in words of falsehood and untruth, the
>   Glory was seen to flee away from him in the shape of a bird. When his
>   Glory had disappeared, then the great Yima . . . , the good shepherd, trem-
>   bled and was in sorrow before his foes; he was confounded, and laid him
>   down on the ground.

Above: Yima's divine glory flew away in the shape of a bird, symbol of Ahura Mazda.

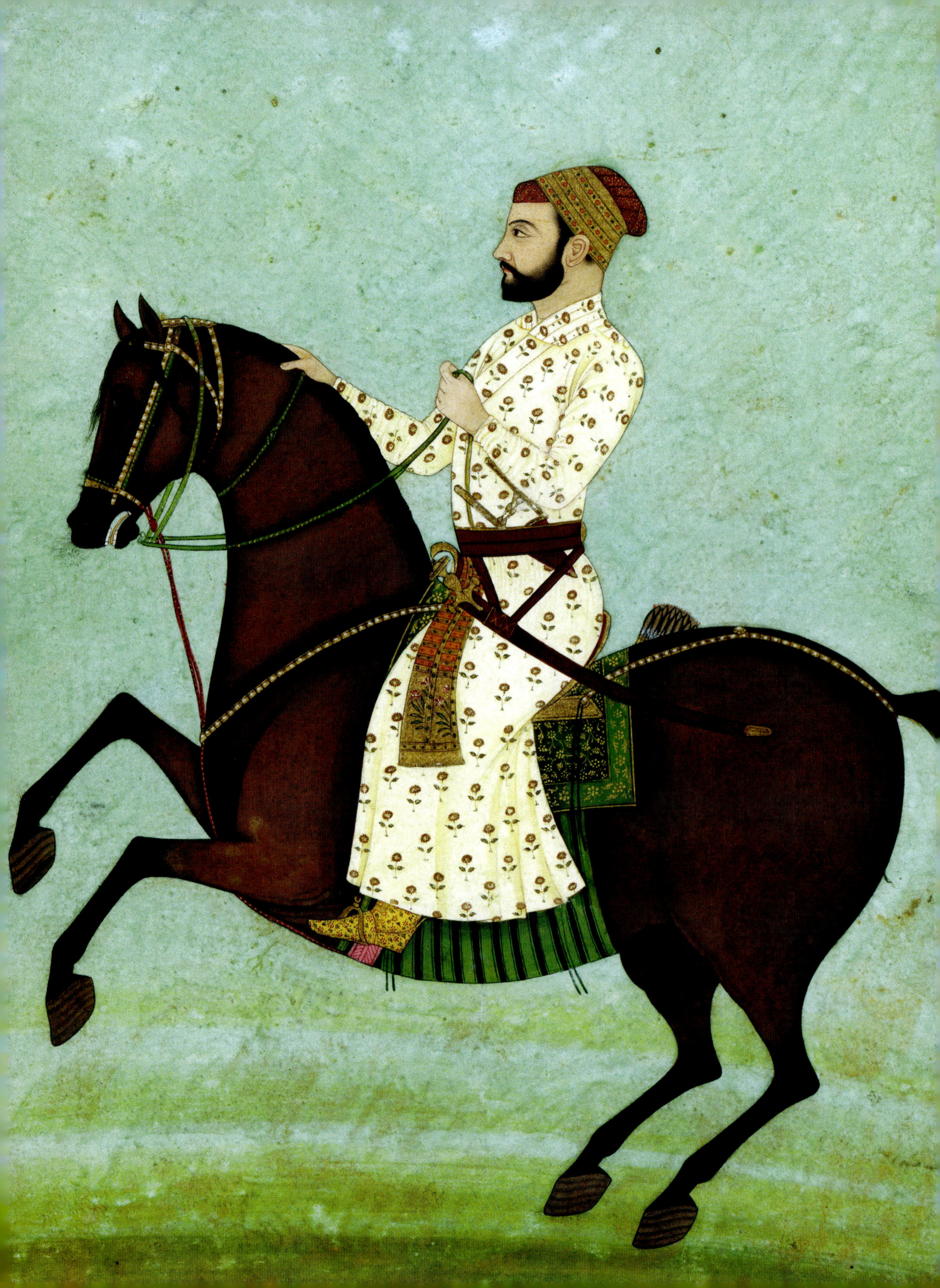

GOOD TRIUMPHS over EVIL

Zahhak the Serpent King

OUR NEXT MYTH TAKES US BACK TO THE IMAGINATIVE version of Persian history found in the *Shahnameh*. In that famous epic poem, Yima is called Jamshid. Jamshid was a great king who was eventually corrupted by his pride and ambition. As a result of his sins, his kingdom fell into chaos. The people of Persia turned to the neighboring kingdom of Arabia for help in overthrowing their wicked ruler. Unfortunately the Arab king was even worse than Jamshid. In fact, King Zahhak was firmly in the clutches of the evil spirit Ahriman.

The stories of Jamshid and Zahhak give us some insight into the ancient Persians' ideas about kingship. The king had a duty to maintain order in society. He was supposed to ensure security, prosperity, and justice for all his subjects. Above all, he should never forget that his powers came directly from God (called Ohrmazd in the New Persian language of the *Shahnameh*). When Jamshid and Zahhak failed in their duties, they lost their God-given *farr*, or divine glory. In time

Opposite: Grace and beauty were not enough to make a man a king. He always had to remember that his powers came from God.

Ohrmazd bestowed the glory on a new hero, Feraydun, who conquered evil and restored order in the world.

These age-old tales of kings and heroes also tell us something about the early Iranians' view of themselves and other peoples. Ferdowsi, the author of the *Shahnameh*, grew up in the mid-900s, about three centuries after the Arab conquest. During this period, the people of Iran were beginning to rediscover and celebrate their ancient heritage. Ferdowsi based his book on ancient Persian mythology, ignoring the traditional stories of Iran's Arab rulers. According to his epic, the first great kings were Persians who ruled over all humanity from their homeland at the center of the world. It was Zahhak, the Arab king, who brought disaster upon the world when he allowed Ahriman to creep into his heart.

CAST *of* CHARACTERS

Jamshid (jam-SHEED) A Persian king; also known as Yima
Merdas (mer-DAHS) A king of Arabia
Zahhak (zah-HAHK) Son of Merdas; an evil king
Ahriman (AH-rih-mun) Spirit of darkness and evil; also known as Angra Mainyu
Eblis (EEB-liss) Ahriman disguised as a nobleman
Ohrmazd (OR-muzd) Supreme god; also known as Ahura Mazda or God
Abetin (ah-beh-TEEN) Father of Feraydun
Tahmures (ta-MOOR-us) Son of Hushang; a Persian king
Feraydun (fur-ay-DOON) A Persian hero and king
Kaveh (KAH-veh) Blacksmith and rebel leader

The Path of Evil

IN THE DAYS when Jamshid sat on the throne of Persia, King Merdas ruled to the south, in the land of the Arabs. Merdas was an honest and generous king who gave freely to his subjects. He was also a righteous man, with a heart dead set against evil.

Merdas had a son named Zahhak. In his youth this handsome prince was as brave and noble as his father. He spent most of his time riding about on his splendid Arab horses, spreading generosity throughout the desert kingdom.

But Zahhak had two great faults: vanity and excessive ambition. Ahriman, lord of evil, searched for a way to take advantage of these failings. Finally, the wicked spirit came up with a plan to replace the good king with his more easily influenced offspring.

> ZAHHAK . . . HAD TEN THOUSAND ARAB HORSES, ALL WITH GOLDEN BRIDLES.
> —THE *SHAHNAMEH*

Ahriman disguised himself as an aged nobleman called Eblis. He went to the royal court, where he used his charming conversation and lavish praise to befriend the unsuspecting prince. Once he had won Zahhak's confidence, the evil one laid his trap. "Your father is old and worn out," he said to the prince. "How long will you remain a wretched subject, when you deserve to be king of the world?"

At first Zahhak refused to listen to such wicked talk. But gradually his pride and ambition overcame his devotion to his father. "Very well," he said. "Tell me how I can gain my rightful throne."

Early the next morning, good king Merdas went to his orchard to pray, as was his custom. Eblis had dug a deep pit in the orchard path.

In the dim light before dawn, the king fell into the hole. The reverent man's back broke, and his life departed.

Zahhak and Eblis quickly erased the evidence of their crime. They recovered the body and placed it in the path, so that it would look like the old king had simply stumbled. They filled in the pit with soil. Then the sinful son placed his father's crown on his head and mounted the golden throne of Arabia.

A Devilish Curse

Zahhak longed to put his terrible crime behind him. He dismissed Eblis from the court and tried to rule with justice and compassion. But Ahriman had other plans. With the young king at his command, the evil spirit was determined to spread suffering throughout the world of humans.

One day an agreeable young stranger presented himself to the king. "I am an excellent cook," said the man. "It would be the greatest of all honors for me to nourish the body of such a noble monarch."

Flattered by these warm words, Zahhak accepted the man into his service. For the next few days, the new cook prepared delicious dishes from the flesh of birds and animals. Partridge and white pheasant meat! Chicken and lamb kebabs! Veal cooked with saffron and rose water! Rubbing his stomach, the delighted king summoned the cook and exclaimed, "Your skill and devotion are truly incredible! What do you desire most in the world? Ask me, and I will grant it."

"I have only one desire," answered the cook. "Although I am quite unworthy, I beg for the privilege of kissing your shoulders."

This was a most unusual request, but the king had given his word. He nodded, and the cook stepped forward. Embracing his master as though they were equals, the man pressed his lips to the royal shoul-

The royal court feasted on the delicacies prepared by the king's mysterious cook.

ders. Suddenly two remarkable things happened. The man—who was really Ahriman in disguise—vanished. And two black snakes began to grow from Zahhak's shoulders.

The king and his court cried out in horror. Zahhak tried to pull off the snakes, but they were stuck as firmly as the limbs on a tree. He hacked them off with his sword, but they grew right back again. He summoned the most learned physicians in the land. The men tried one remedy after another. Still the monstrous serpents writhed and twisted on the king's shoulders.

Then Ahriman appeared once more, this time in the guise of a wise old doctor. "There is only way to get rid of these growths," the evil spirit said solemnly. "You must feed them human brains. Give them nothing but brains to eat, and in time they will sicken and die."

From then on, two young men were dragged to the palace each morning. The victims were killed, and their brains were fed to the snakes. But the hissing monsters showed no signs of dying, and Zahhak the serpent king fell ever more deeply under Ahriman's power.

Zahhak the Serpent King | 63

Feraydun the Hero

Each day two unfortunate men were sacrificed to feed the serpents on Zahhak's shoulders.

While the people of the Arab lands suffered, a dark cloud was also gathering over Persia. Jamshid, once the most splendid of kings, had fallen into pride and falsehood. When the foolish king proclaimed himself equal to Ohrmazd, the great god withdrew Jamshid's divine glory. Petty lords sprang up on all sides, challenging the king's authority. The land was plunged into war as the contenders battled over who had the greater right to the throne. Finally, a group of Persian nobles made their way to the court of Arabia's famous serpent king. The desperate men begged the powerful monarch to liberate them from their oppressive ruler and restore peace to their land.

Zahhak eagerly accepted the mission. Swift as the wind, he rode north with an army of Persians and Arabs. He captured the despised Persian king and had him sawed in two. Thus the reign of Jamshid came to an end, and Zahhak became king of the whole world.

The Persians soon learned to regret their choice of ruler. Under the reign of Zahhak, goodness hid its face and wickedness flourished throughout the world. The king erected idols to false gods. He burned many cities and villages. He murdered many innocent people, including the two young men sacrificed each day to provide his serpents with their evil nourishment.

One night Ohrmazd sent a dream to trouble the wicked ruler. In his vision Zahhak saw a tall, shining warrior. The young man hit him over the head with an ox-headed mace and dragged him from the palace. Waking with a scream, the king sent for his priests and sorcerers. The learned men shook their heads and gave Zahhak the news he was dreading: the dream was a sign that a young hero was coming to seize the throne.

From that day on, Zahhak could hardly sleep or eat for terror. He commanded his warriors to scour the world for the coming hero. Many more innocent people were slaughtered. Among the victims was a man named Abetin, who was descended from Tahmures, the great king known as the Binder of Demons.

Abetin's wife had just given birth to a boy named Feraydun. When her husband was killed, the woman fled north with her son. The child grew up in the Alborz Mountains, safely hidden from the king's assassins. He grew as tall and straight as a cypress tree, and all who saw him marveled at the royal splendor that shined from his face like the sun.

When Feraydun was sixteen years old, he asked his mother about his family. The bold young man's heart filled with pain and fury as he heard the story of his father's murder. He longed to rush straight to the palace and confront the evil monarch. Only his mother's pleading stopped him. The woman wept bitter tears and begged her son not to throw his life away. At last Feraydun agreed to delay his attack until he could gather enough followers to challenge Zahhak's powerful army.

Feraydun's devoted mother protected her son from the evil serpent king.

Zahhak the Serpent King | 65

The End of a Tyrant

Feraydun would not have to wait long for his vengeance. At the very moment that he made his pledge to his mother, an extraordinary confrontation was taking place at the royal palace. Zahhak was holding audience when a lowly blacksmith named Kaveh suddenly strode into the throne room. Kaveh's beloved son was about to be killed to feed the king's serpents. Shaking his fist, the blacksmith demanded that the boy be freed.

Zahhak nearly ordered his guards to seize the insolent commoner. Then a strange vision appeared before his eyes. A mountain of iron, tall and forbidding, seemed to rise up before Kaveh. Filled with foreboding, the shaken king meekly agreed to the blacksmith's demands.

Kaveh and his son marched straight from the palace to the busy marketplace. There the blacksmith hoisted his leather apron on a spear as a rallying point. "Today it was my boy. Tomorrow it will be yours," he shouted. "This evil king is Ahriman himself. We must free ourselves from Zahhak's chains."

A crowd of people quickly gathered around the leather banner, roaring their approval. Kaveh marched his men from the city and through the countryside, gathering more and more followers as they went along. He led his ragged army all the way to the mountains, where the heir of Tahmures was waiting.

Feraydun welcomed the army warmly. He took the humble leather flag and adorned it with brilliant jewels. He asked the blacksmith to make him a mace in the form of a massive ox head. Raising his weapon to the heavens, the noble youth set off to avenge his father.

The warriors raced across the mountains and valleys. Soon the walls of the palace loomed before them. The hero raised his mace, and holy fire seemed to burst forth from his body. Urging his horse forward, he let forth a thunderous cry. The rebel army stormed the palace, crushing all of Zahhak's sorcerers and demons and overturning all the false idols.

At last Feraydun faced Zahhak in single combat. The serpent king leapt at his challenger with a glittering dagger. The hero brought his mace crashing down on Zahhak's head, shattering the king's helmet. He was about to deliver the killing blow when an angel of Ohrmazd appeared. "Do not strike him again," said the shining messenger. "Bind him and take him to the mountains."

So Feraydun bound Zahhak's arms and legs with strips of lion skin. He dragged the wretched captive to Mount Damavand. There Zahhak was imprisoned in a deep, dark cave, where he would suffer until the end of time.

Then Feraydun returned to the palace and ascended the throne. The whole earth rejoiced at the overthrow of Zahhak and the rise of the brave new king. For the next five hundred years, Feraydun would rule over a world free from evil, and all the people would enjoy peace and good fortune.

> **FERAYDUN RAISED HIS OX-HEADED MACE TO SLAY THE SERPENT-KING.**
> —THE *SHAHNAMEH*

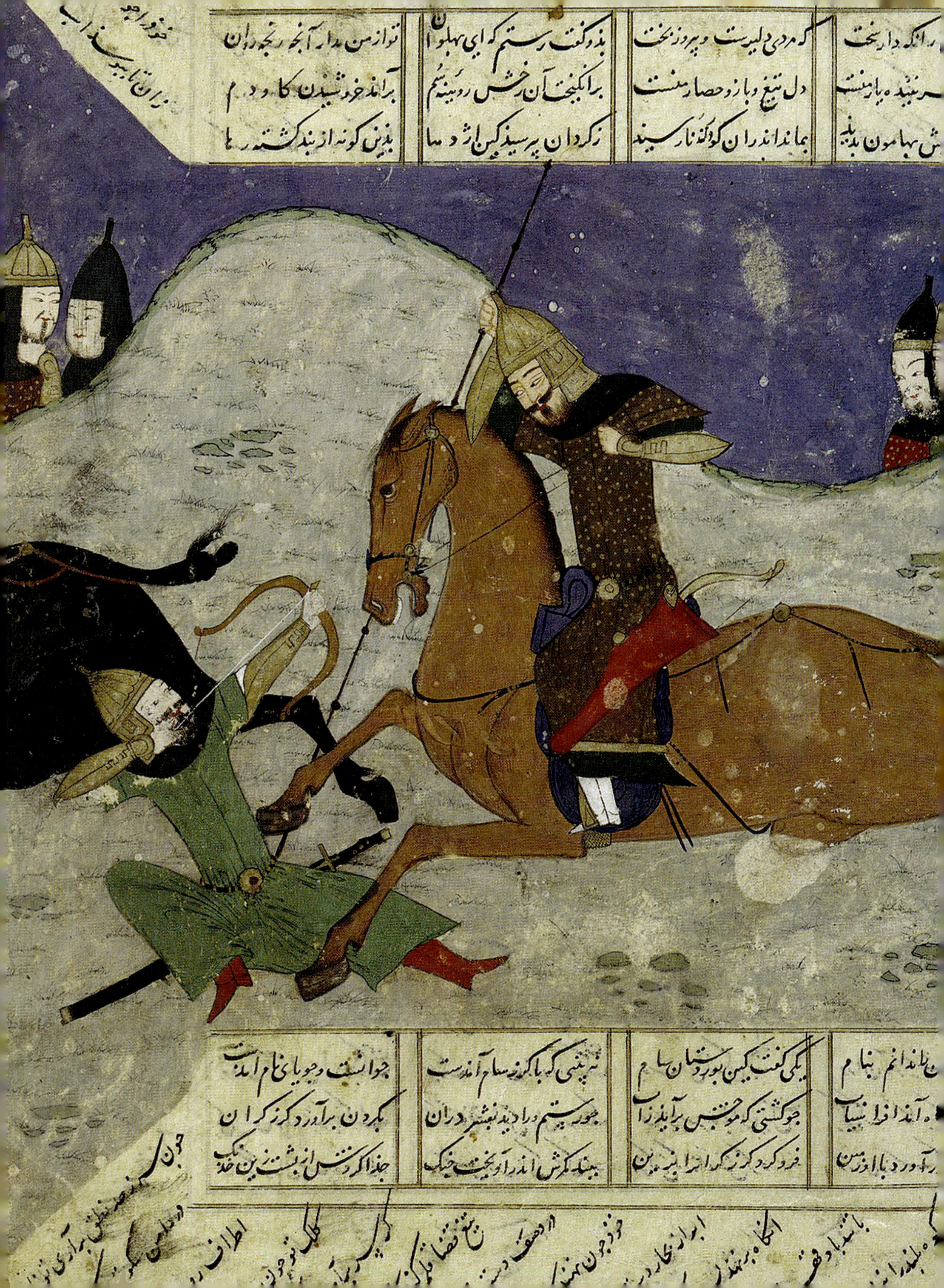

که مردی دلیرست و پیروزبخت
دل تیغ و بازو حصار منست
بدو گفت رستم که ای پهلوان
برانگیخت آن رخش رویینه سم
ز گردان بپرسید کین اژدها
تو از من مدار آنچه رنج روان
بدین گونه از بند گشته رها
یکی گفت کین پور دستان سام
چو کشتی که موج اندر آید ز آب
نه پیچی که با گرز سام آمدست
چو رستم ورا دید بفشرد ران
جوانست و جویای نام آمدست
بگردن برآورد گرز گران

MYTHICAL CREATURES

Rostam and His Marvelous Horse

MANY INCREDIBLE CREATURES POPULATE THE WORLD of ancient Persian mythology. There are fearsome dragons, demons, and monsters. There are also friendly beasts that use their magical powers to protect Persia and its heroes. One of the most famous of these helpful mythical creatures is Rakhsh. This magnificent horse was said to have the strength of an elephant and the speed of a racing camel. His courage, intelligence, and loyalty made him the perfect partner for the greatest of all Persian heroes, Rostam.

According to Ferdowsi's *Shahnameh*, Rostam lived in the turbulent days following the reign of Feraydun. The good king's death had led to a long period of war and upheaval. Over several centuries the Persians fought a series of battles with the northern kingdom of Turan.* Rostam was the foremost champion on the Persians' side. With the help of his brave and faithful horse Rakhsh, he spent his life defending his country against invading armies, dangerous demons, and other perils.

*Turan was an ancient region in central Asia, north of the Oxus River; its exact location is unknown.

Opposite: Rostam and his fabulous horse Rakhsh defended the kingdom from invaders.

Most of the stories in the *Shahnameh* are based on ancient tales that had also been told in the Avesta, the Zoroastrian holy book created many centuries earlier. However, Rostam was never mentioned in the Avesta. His adventures seem to have belonged to another set of traditional stories, which originated in a different part of Persia. These tales were so popular that Ferdowsi decided to work them into his grand chronicle of Persian history. Whatever the origins of Rostam, countless generations of Iranians have celebrated him as the ideal example of strength, courage, virtue, and devotion to country.

CAST *of* CHARACTERS

Rostam (roos-TAM) The champion of Persia

Feraydun (fur-ay-DOON) A Persian hero and king

Afrasyab (ah-frah-SEE-yahb) A prince of Turan

Zal A Persian warrior; father of Rostam

Rakhsh (raxsh) Rostam's horse

Akvan (AK-vahn) A famous demon

Kay Khosrow (kay KOOS-row) A Persian king

Ahriman (AH-rih-mun) Spirit of darkness and evil; also known as Angra Mainyu

A Horse Fit for a Hero

FROM THE DAY of his birth, Rostam was marked for greatness. He was such a large infant that he could not be born in the usual manner. Instead, a priest had to cut open his sleeping mother to bring him into the world. When the woman awoke, she smiled at the sight of her noble child, whose face shined like the sun and the evening star together.

Rostam grew up in troubled times. Following the death of Feraydun, the kingdom of the Persians had suffered under one weak king after another. Eager to take advantage of the confusion, the king of Turan sent his son Afrasyab to seize his neighbor's throne. As the Turanian prince led his army south, the Persians turned to Zal, the great warrior who had served as their country's loyal champion under four kings. And Zal, whose back was bent with age, turned to his noble son Rostam.

"You have grown as tall as a cypress tree," said Zal, "yet you are still a boy. How can I ask you to take on the task of a seasoned warrior when your heart still yearns for the pleasures of youth?"

Rostam answered Zal: "Wine, feasting, and comfort mean nothing to me. All I ask is to fight our country's foes. But I will need a warhorse strong and brave if I am to defend Persia."

The young hero's words filled his father's heart with pride. Zal swiftly dispatched men throughout the kingdom, searching for a steed fit for his son. Great herds were driven before

Rostam was cut from his mother's belly, in the first-ever cesarean birth.

Rostam and His Marvelous Horse

Rostam. Whenever he saw a fine horse, the towering youth pressed the palm of his hand against its back. Each time, the animal's belly sagged to the ground. Not one of the horses was strong enough to bear the weight of such a mighty hero.

At last a large gray mare galloped by. Behind the mare came a remarkable black-eyed foal. The young horse had a chest as broad as a lion's. Its lustrous gold-and-red coat sparkled like jewels in the sun. It held its tail high and ran faster than a racing camel on its hooves of iron.

> [ROSTAM] MADE A RUNNING KNOT IN HIS CORD AND . . . CAUGHT THE COLT IN THE SNARE.
> —THE *SHAHNAMEH*

Quickly the hero flung his lasso over the foal's head. The mother horse came charging to her young one's defense. As she opened her mouth to bite Rostam, the young man roared like a lion. The thunderous sound stopped the mare in her tracks. Turning in terror, she scrambled off to rejoin her herd.

Rostam pulled the foal close, calming it with gentle words. He pushed down on its back with all his strength, but the horse stood firm. "Who owns this magnificent foal?" he asked.

The herdsman who had brought the horses answered: "My lord, no one knows who owns him. For two years he has run wild among my horses, and no one has been able to capture him. All I know is that he has always been called Rostam's Rakhsh."

"I am Rostam. What is the price of the foal?"

"If you are indeed Rostam, the price is Persia itself," replied the man. "Take him and defend our land from its enemies."

So Rostam set a saddle on Rakhsh. The swift and powerful horse took off like a magical creature, carrying his rider across the land. Everywhere the hero and his marvelous horse went, they inspired the people to take arms against Persia's foes.

Rostam Outsmarts a Demon

Rostam triumphed over all his enemies, including a fierce monster known as the White Demon.

Together Rostam and Rakhsh had many adventures and faced many deadly perils. They fought a ferocious lion, a hideous witch, and a fire-breathing dragon. They nearly died of thirst crossing a waterless desert. They battled Prince Afrasyab, hurling him from his saddle and forcing his army to flee back to Turan.

Rostam also fought many dangerous demons. His battle against the dreadful demon Akvan came during the reign of Kay Khosrow. One day a herdsman came to the royal court, asking the king for help. "A wild ass has appeared in my herd," the man reported. "It chases the horses and breaks their necks with a snap of its powerful jaws."

Khosrow knew that no wild ass could be stronger than a horse. He decided to send Rostam to deal with the mysterious animal. "Go and fight this creature," the king commanded. "But be careful, for it may be Ahriman himself, who is always looking for ways to harm us mortals."

Rostam and His Marvelous Horse | 73

At once Rostam rode out to the plains. He saw the creature racing over the ground like the north wind. The ugly beast had a head as big as an elephant's and a mouth full of boar's tusks. When Rostam galloped near, it disappeared right before his eyes. That was when the hero knew that he was dealing with Akvan, the dangerous demon who could take the form of any animal and had the power of invisibility.

For three days and nights, Rostam pursued his quarry. Each time he came close enough to shoot his bow, the demon simply vanished. At last the hero was so exhausted that he lay down beside a stream. The moment he fell asleep, Akvan attacked. The monster transformed itself into a storm wind and scooped up the hero. Rostam awoke to find himself whirling around in the sky. "Make a wish, mighty hero!" the demon shouted with an evil laugh. "Shall I throw you into the ocean to drown or hurl you to your death on a mountaintop?"

> [THE DEMON] FLUNG [ROSTAM] INTO THE SEA AT A SPOT WHERE HUNGRY CROCODILES WOULD DEVOUR HIM.
>
> —THE *SHAHNAMEH*

Rostam had to think quickly. He knew that his bones would be smashed if he were dropped on a mountain, while he had a chance to

74 *The* ANCIENT PERSIANS

survive in the ocean. At the same time, he suspected that the cruel demon would turn his wishes upside down. So he begged his enemy to throw him to earth—and just as he had expected, Akvan flung him into the sea.

The hero drew his sword as he plunged into the watery depths. He rose to the surface, only to find himself surrounded by hungry sharks and sea monsters. With his right arm, he fended off the fierce creatures. With his left arm and his legs, he swam. Drawing on his great strength, he finally made it to dry land.

Once he had rested, Rostam rode his faithful horse back to the stream where he had encountered Akvan. The demon was so astonished to see the young warrior alive and well that it forgot to make itself invisible. Quickly Rostam flung his lasso, capturing the monster. He raised his mace like a blacksmith's hammer. Then he brought the heavy weapon down with a powerful blow, smashing Akvan's skull to bits.

After his great victory, Rostam returned to the court of Kay Khosrow. The king and all his nobles sang the praises of the hero who had set out to capture a wild ass and ended up defeating a demon. Two weeks passed in merry feasting, songs, and storytelling. Then the champion of Persia mounted his marvelous horse and rode off in search of new adventures.

THE EARLY PERSIANS SPEAK
The KING of BIRDS

Along with the fabulous horse Rakhsh, another mythical creature played an important role in Rostam's life: the Simorgh. According to ancient tales that were eventually preserved in the *Shahnameh*, this mysterious bird lived high in the Alborz Mountains. The Simorgh raised Rostam's father, Zal, after he was abandoned in the mountains as an infant. When Zal was grown, the "king of birds" gave him a magical feather. The man used the feather to summon the Simorgh in times of need, including the day when Rostam and his horse were mortally wounded in battle.

Above: The colorful Simorgh was one of the most mysterious creatures of Persian mythology.

Zal . . . drew a feather from its brocade wrapping; fanning the flames in one of the braziers [containers for fire] he burnt a portion of the feather in the fire. One watch of the night passed, and suddenly the air turned much darker. Zal peered into the night, and it seemed as if the fire and the Simorgh's flight were liquefying the air: then he caught sight of the Simorgh and the flames flared up. . . . The Simorgh said to him:

"O king, explain to me what you desire
That you have summoned me in smoke and fire."

Zal answered: ". . . The lionhearted Rostam lies grievously wounded, and my feet feel as though shackled by his sorrows. No man has ever seen such wounds and we despair of his life. And it seems that Rakhsh too will die from the arrow heads that torment him. . . ."

The bird examined Rostam's wounds, looking for how they could be healed. With his beak he sucked blood from the lesions, and drew out eight arrow heads. Then he pressed one of his feathers against the wounds, and immediately Rostam's spirits began to return. The Simorgh said, "Bind up your wounds and keep them safe from further injury for seven days: then soak one of my feathers in milk and place it on the scars to help them heal." He treated Rakhsh in the same manner, using his beak to draw out six arrow heads from the horse's neck, and immediately Rakhsh neighed loudly, and Rostam laughed for joy.

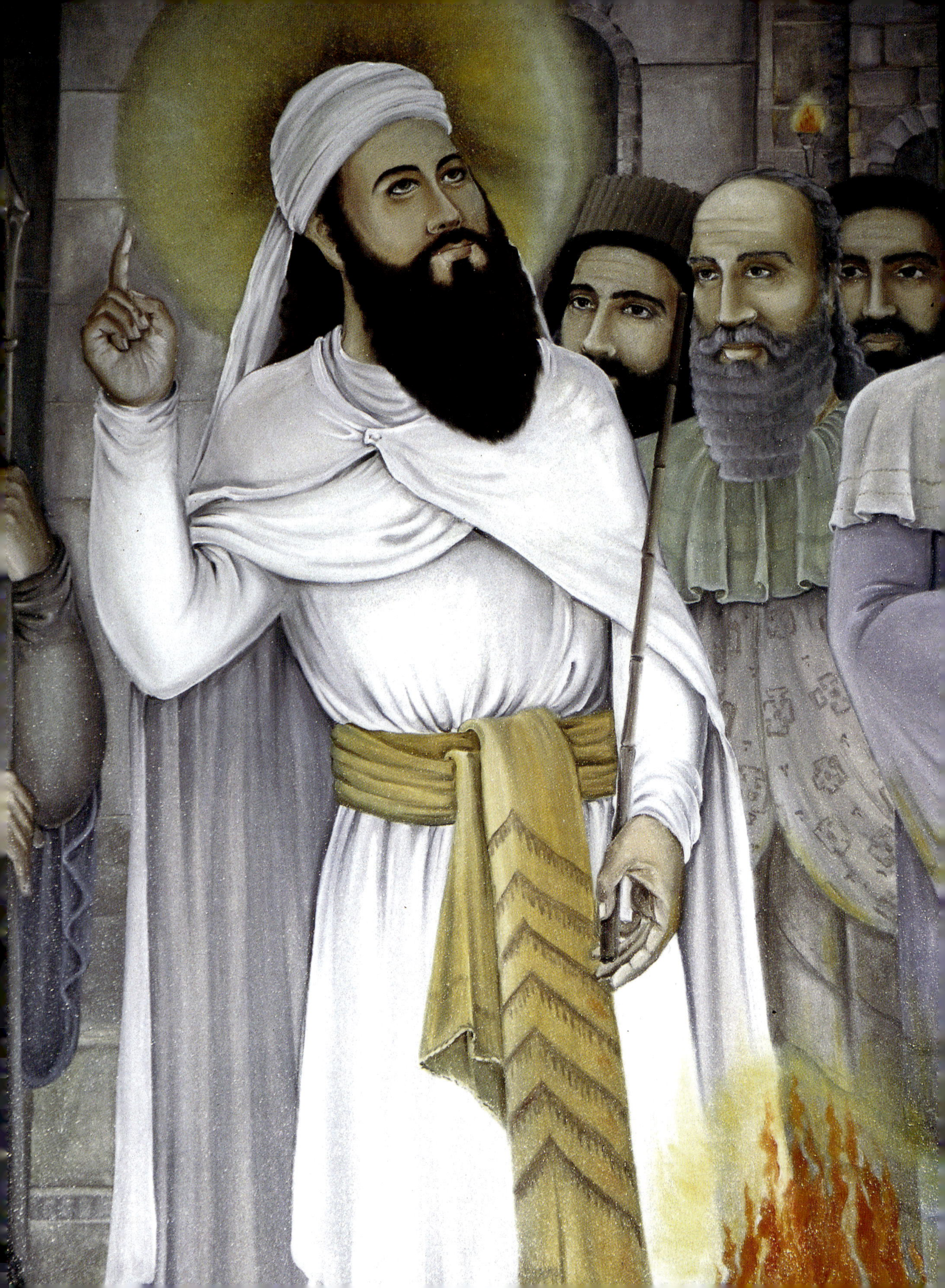

THE FOUNDING of ZOROASTRIANISM

The Life of Zarathustra

VERY LITTLE IS KNOWN ABOUT ZARATHUSTRA (ALSO known as Zardosht or Zoroaster), the prophet who founded the dominant religion of the ancient Persian Empire. Modern-day scholars have pieced together an outline of his life from ancient sources that offer a confusing blend of history, religion, and mythology. These include the *Gathas*, a set of hymns believed to have been composed by the prophet himself, and the Pahlavi texts, religious books written centuries later by the followers of Zoroastrianism.

According to clues found in these sources, Zarathustra may have lived in central Asia sometime between 1800 and 1500 BCE. As a young man, he served as a priest of his tribe's age-old religion. At some point he had a mystical vision of Ahura Mazda. In this vision, Ahura Mazda revealed the principles of a religion based on the belief in one supreme god, rather than many different gods. Zarathustra devoted the rest of his life to spreading the word about this new faith.

Opposite: Zarathustra built a new religion on the foundations of his people's ancient beliefs.

Following Zarathustra's death, the story of his life was told and retold by his followers. Gradually, the figure of Zarathustra became the hero of a sacred tale with many fantastic elements. According to that tale, the coming of the prophet was foretold from the beginning of the world. Miracles surrounded the birth of his mother as well as his own birth and childhood. As he carried out his divine mission, he faced threats from both human opponents and evil demons. He overcame all these obstacles with the help of his great wisdom and the miraculous powers granted to him by Ahura Mazda.

The sacred account of Zarathustra's life has inspired generations of Zoroastrians, from ancient times through the present day. In this well-loved narrative, the prophet serves as an example of the ideal man, who remains steadfast in his faith despite all trials and temptations. His story is a call for his followers to remain equally faithful and courageous. It is also a promise that the forces of goodness will ultimately triumph over evil.

CAST *of* CHARACTERS

Zarathustra (zuh-rah-THOOSH-truh) Prophet and founder of Zoroastrianism; also known as Zardosht or Zoroaster

Ahura Mazda (ah-HOOR-uh MAZ-duh) Supreme god; also known as Ohrmazd or God

Dughdhova (DUGH-doe-vuh) Mother of Zarathustra

Angra Mainyu (ANG-ruh MUN-yoo) Spirit of darkness and evil; also known as Ahriman

Pourushaspa (POOR-uh-shas-pa) Earthly father of Zarathustra

Vohu Manah (VOH-uh MA-nah) An Amesha Spenta, or angel-like being

Vishtaspa (VISH-tas-pa) Ruler of a kingdom in central Asia

The Birth of Zarathustra

When it was nearly time for Zarathustra to come into the world, Ahura Mazda sent the light of the sun, moon, and stars down to earth. The divine glory entered the fire burning in the home of a man and his wife. From the fire, the radiance flew on into the wife's body. Time passed, and the woman gave birth to a baby girl named Dughdhova. And that little girl, who was destined to become the mother of the prophet, shined with a light brighter than any fire.

The demons who serve Angra Mainyu knew that the divine glory could mean their downfall. Hoping to injure Dughdhova, they afflicted her village with bitter winters, deadly diseases, and other catastrophes. They whispered that the young girl with the mysterious light was the cause of all these hardships. The rumors that they started spread through the village, and Dughdhova's father was forced to send his daughter to live with a far-off family. But the angels watched over the poor maiden. They guided her safely to her new home. They also made sure that her new family included a young man named Pourushaspa, who was fated to become her husband.

Soon the young bride conceived a child. Three days before the baby's birth, the village began to glow like the sky just before the dawn. The whole world held its breath. Then Zarathustra was born, and all the animals, plants, and waters of the Good Creation rejoiced.

Meanwhile, in the home of the new parents, the midwives gasped at the sight of the radiant man-child. The remarkable infant did not cry like other babies. He laughed out loud, for he was already aware of his glorious mission on earth.

Marvels and Miracles

When Zarathustra was still a child, the demons tried again and again to destroy him. Using their evil powers, they twisted Pourushaspa's mind until he believed that his son's radiant glory was a sign of the devil. In his madness the father placed the infant on a pile of wood. He set the wood on fire, but the crackling flames refused to touch the boy. Next the deluded man laid Zarathustra in the path of a stampeding herd of oxen. One old ox stood guard over the baby until the danger was past. Then Pourushaspa left his son in the den of a fierce she-wolf. Instead of attacking the boy, the wolf cared for him like one of her own cubs.

> **[ZARATHUSTRA] SAW THE ARCHANGEL VOHU MANAH IN THE FORM OF A MAN, HANDSOME, BRILLIANT, AND ELEGANT.**
> —THE *WIZIDAGIHA*

Zarathustra survived these and many other attempts on his life. He grew into a fine young man known far and wide for his wisdom and virtue. By the age of thirty, he had become a respected priest of the old religion. But his heart still longed for a higher truth and greater righteousness.

One morning Zarathustra went to the river to fill his jug for a sacred ritual. As he emerged from the waters, he saw a tall figure clothed in pure sunlight. "Who are you?" asked the awestruck priest.

"I am Vohu Manah ('Good Thought'). Come with me, O

seeker of righteousness, and I will take you to the One who created you."

So the young priest followed the angel up into the blue sky. They climbed to a place where the light was so brilliant that at first Zarathustra was blinded. Then his vision cleared, and he beheld the Amesha Spentas and the supreme lord and creator, Ahura Mazda.

Zarathustra listened reverently as the divinities instructed him in the good religion. They told the young man that there was only one true god, the creator of all the good things in the universe. They taught him about the eternal struggle between good and evil. "I have chosen you to carry my divine word to the people," said Ahura Mazda. "Teach them how to live righteous lives. Teach them the power of good thoughts, good words, and good deeds." Then the supreme god gave his prophet powerful prayers and spells for protection against the forces of darkness.

The prophet returned from the heavens with the words of Ahura Mazda.

For the next few years, Zarathustra traveled about the land, preaching the word of Ahura Mazda. Many nobles and priests condemned the prophet whose teachings threatened the old order. Many demons tried to kill him or to tempt him away from righteousness. All their efforts were in vain. Zarathustra remained resolute in his faith. He confounded his human enemies with his wisdom and shattered the demons with his God-given spells. Whenever he grew weary of his struggles, Ahura Mazda sent another divine vision and granted him the strength to carry on with his mission.

The Life of Zarathustra

Zarathustra gained a valuable convert when he miraculously healed King Vishtaspa's favorite stallion.

After ten years of preaching, Zarathustra finally made his first important convert: King Vishtaspa. Jealous priests and counselors had convinced the powerful eastern ruler that the prophet was an evil sorcerer. Vishtaspa had thrown Zarathustra into his deepest dungeon. Then a miracle occurred. The king's favorite horse was stricken with a mysterious disease that left its legs bent and paralyzed. The prophet sent word that he would heal the animal, under four conditions: Vishtaspa must accept the new religion, his queen must also convert, his son must fight for the faith, and the names of the plotters must be revealed. One by one the king agreed to the conditions. One by one the stallion's legs unbent, until the animal was prancing about once again.

Following that miracle, the king and all his court accepted the good religion. Zarathustra's heavenly teachings spread throughout the kingdom and on to other lands and other peoples. The faithful prophet lived to the age of seventy-seven, when he was murdered by an unbeliever. Even after his death, the fire of the religion that he founded would continue to burn brightly through the centuries.

THE EARLY PERSIANS SPEAK
The END of EVIL

Zoroastrians believe that the final period of world history began when Ahura Mazda (or Ohrmazd) revealed the good religion to Zarathustra. This period will last for three thousand years. Toward the end of that time, the whole world will be engulfed in the epic struggle between good and evil. Then a final savior named Soshyant will appear. Soshyant will be the son of Zarathustra, miraculously conceived long after the prophet's death. He will summon all people, living and dead, to a last judgment. The good will go to heaven. The wicked will go to hell, where they will be purified in a river of fire. The angels will vanquish all the demons, Ahura Mazda will destroy the evil spirit Angra Mainyu (or Ahriman) once and for all, and all people will dwell forever in God's divine kingdom. This passage from a ninth-century text called the *Denkard* describes these earth-shattering events, which Zoroastrians call the Renovation.

> The man Soshyant is born whose food is spiritual and body sunny [as radiant as the sun]. . . .
>
> In fifty-seven of his years there occur the annihilation of the fiendishness of the two-legged race and others, and the subjugation [conquest] of disease and decrepitude [weakness], of death and persecution, and of the original evil of tyranny, apostasy [renouncing of religion], and depravity; there arise a perpetual verdant [green] growth of vegetation and the primitive gift of joyfulness. . . .
>
> And all mankind remain of one accord in the religion of Ohrmazd, owing to the will of the creator [and] the command of that apostle. . . .
>
> At the end of the fifty-seven years the fiend [Az, demon of lust] and Ahriman are annihilated, the renovation for the future existence occurs, and the whole of the good creation is provided with purity and perfect splendour.

Above: A scene of the last judgment, painted in nineteenth-century Iran

GLOSSARY

Achaemenid (uh-KEE-muh-nud) one of the greatest dynasties of ancient Persia, named for the family's legendary founder, Achaemenes; Achaemenid kings ruled from the time of Cyrus the Great in the sixth century BCE to the overthrow of Darius III in 330 BCE

Amesha Spentas six (or sometimes seven) immortal beings created by Ahura Mazda, who are similar to angels and represent qualities of the creator, such as "Good Thought" and "Holy Devotion"; *Amesha Spenta* means "Bounteous Immortal" or "Holy Immortal"

Aryans (AH-ree-unz) a nomadic people originating in central Asia, who migrated into the Iranian plateau after 1800 BCE; the word *Iran* is a later form of *Aryan*

deities gods, goddesses, and other divine beings

dynasty a ruling family that passes down its authority from generation to generation

epic poem a long narrative poem celebrating the deeds of mythical, legendary, or historical beings

farr a radiant light and protection bestowed by God (Ahura Mazda or Ohrmazd) on a king or great hero; *farr* is often translated as "divine glory"

fravashis the immortal spirits of men and women, which serve as warriors in the cosmic battle against evil; according to Zoroastrian beliefs, every living person has both an internal soul, which can choose either good or evil, and a heavenly *fravashi*, which cannot be corrupted

imperial relating to an emperor or empire

legend a traditional story that may involve ordinary mor-

A ram and ewe from a miniature painting

86 | *The* ANCIENT PERSIANS

tals as well as divine beings and may be partly based on real people and events

mace a heavy club used as a weapon

magi (MAY-jie) the priests of ancient Persia; the singular form is *magus*. To many Westerners, the best-known magi are the "three kings of Orient," who are said to have followed a star to the birthplace of Jesus Christ.

mythology the whole body of myths belonging to a people

myths traditional stories about gods and other divine and semi-divine beings, which were developed by ancient cultures to explain the mysteries of the physical and spiritual worlds

nomads people who move from place to place in search of food, water, and grazing land

Sassanians (suh-SAH-nee-enz) members of a Persian dynasty that founded the second great Persian Empire; Sassanian kings ruled from 224 to 651 CE

scribes educated people who kept official records, wrote personal letters, and performed other writing jobs for a living

vara an enclosure or cavern

yazatas angelic spirits who serve as divine warriors in the battle against evil; *yazatas* means "spirits worthy of worship"

ANCIENT PERSIAN WRITING *and* TEXTS

Much of our information about ancient Persian myths comes from the religious texts of the followers of Zoroastrianism. These texts were memorized and passed down orally by priests for many centuries. Scribes finally began to write them down

Priests at a Zoroastrian fire altar adorn a Sassanian coin.

around the sixth century CE, under the Sassanians, rulers of the last Persian Empire. The myths in this book are drawn mainly from the texts described below.

The Avesta is the holy book of Zoroastrianism. It is made up a variety of sacred texts, some dating back nearly four thousand years. The present-day Avesta has five main parts:

- The *Yasna*. The most important and sacred section, which includes the *Gathas*, seventeen hymns that are believed to have been composed by Zarathustra himself.
- The *Yasht*. Hymns in praise of Ahura Mazda and the major *yazatas*.
- The *Vendidad*. The priestly code of Zoroastrianism, with rules for physical and spiritual purity. "Yima Saves the World" (page 51) is based mainly on the *Vendidad*.
- The *Khordeh Avesta* ("Shorter Avesta"). Short prayers for the common people to use.
- The *Visperad*. Additional prayers and hymns, recited by priests during special services.

The Pahlavi Texts are collections of ancient Zoroastrian myths and religious knowledge, which were written mainly in the ninth century CE, two centuries after the Arab conquest. Following the fall of the Persian Empire, many Iranians had lost faith in their old religion and converted to Islam. Zoroastrian priests and scholars compiled the Pahlavi texts in order to comfort and inspire the faithful in this time of crisis. The name *Pahlavi* comes from the language of the texts, which is also called Middle Persian.

Three Pahlavi books are important sources of information on ancient Persian beliefs and myths:

- The *Denkard* ("Acts of Religion") is a collection of ancient myths and religious knowledge, including a summary of the Avesta in the Pahlavi language.
- The *Bundahishn* ("Book of Original Creation") traces the history of the world from the creation to the end of time.
- The *Wizidagiha* ("Selections") includes excerpts from the Avesta on themes including the creation, the life of Zarathustra, and the world-ending event known as the Renovation. This text was written by a Zoroastrian priest named Zadspram, who lived in the late ninth century CE.

"Ahura Mazda and the Good Creation" (page 31) is based largely on the *Bundahishn*. Our two main sources for "The Life of Zarathustra" (page 79) are the *Denkard* and the *Wizidagiha*.

The *Shahnameh*, or "Book of Kings," is the national epic of Iran. It was written in the New Persian language (also called Farsi) at the turn of the tenth and eleventh centuries CE by a poet from eastern Iran known as Ferdowsi. Ferdowsi based his famous epic poem on oral and written sources dating back to the earliest days of Persian history. His book tells the story of hundreds of kings, from the first mythical rulers through the real-life shahs who ruled over Iran in the period leading up to the Arab conquest. The *Shahnameh* is regarded as one of the world's greatest works of literature, as well as a valuable source of information on ancient Persian customs, values, beliefs, and myths. It is the main source for three of the stories retold in this book: "The First Earthly Kings" (page 41), "Zahhak the Serpent King" (page 59), and "Rostam and His Marvelous Horse" (page 69).

To FIND OUT MORE

BOOKS AND ARTICLES

Barter, James. *The Ancient Persians*. San Diego, CA: Lucent Books, 2006.

Bramwell, Neil D. *Ancient Persia*. Berkeley Heights, NJ: Enslow, 2004.

Choksy, Jamsheed K. "Zoroastrianism." In vol. 14 of *Encyclopedia of Religion*. 2nd ed. New York: Macmillan, 2005.

Habeeb, William Mark. *Iran*. Philadelphia: Mason Crest, 2004.

Hartz, Paula R. *Zoroastrianism*. New York: Facts on File, 2004.

Leeming, David. *The Oxford Companion to World Mythology*. New York: Oxford University Press, 2005.

Nardo, Don. *The Persian Empire*. San Diego, CA: Lucent Books, 1998.

Spencer, Lauren. *Iran: A Primary Source Cultural Guide*. New York: Rosen, 2004.

Zeinert, Karen. *The Persian Empire*. New York: Benchmark Books, 1997.

"Zoroastrianism." *Calliope*, January 2005.

WEB SITES

Avesta: Zoroastrian Archives at
http://www.avesta.org
This searchable site offers a complete translation of the Avesta and many other sacred Zoroastrian texts.

Encyclopedia Mythica: Persian Mythology at
http://www.pantheon.org/areas/mythology/middle_east/persian

This online encyclopedia offers more than one hundred brief articles on ancient Persian gods, goddesses, heroes, and other mythical beings.

Forgotten Empire: The World of Ancient Persia at
http://www.thebritishmuseum.ac.uk/forgottenempire
Follow the links to explore the history, government, art, architecture, religion, and legacy of the Persian Empire. This handsome Web site hosted by the British Museum is illustrated with works of art from the museum's collection.

History for Kids: Zoroastrianism at
http://www.historyforkids.org/learn/westasia/religion/zoroastrianism.htm
History for Kids offers a clear, easy-to-read explanation of Zoroastrianism, with links to information on the ancient Persians, the god Ahura Mazda, and other related topics. The site is run by Dr. Karen Carr, Associate Professor of History at Portland State University in Portland, Oregon.

The Internet Classics Archive: The Epic of Kings at
http://classics.mit.edu/Ferdowsi/kings.html
Read about the mythical early rulers of ancient Persia in this online edition of the *Shahnameh*, ancient Persia's "Book of Kings." The text is based on a translation by Helen Zimmern.

Zoroastrian Kids Korner at
http://www.zoroastriankids.com
Learn about Zoroastrian beliefs and life in ancient Persia. This colorful site also offers stories, word games, and crafts.

SELECTED BIBLIOGRAPHY

Allan, Tony, Charles Phillips, and Michael Kerrigan. *Wise Lord of the Sky: Persian Myth*. London: Duncan Baird, 1999.

Boyce, Mary. *Zoroastrians: Their Religious Beliefs and Practices*. Boston: Routledge and Kegan Paul, 1985.

Briant, Pierre. *From Cyrus to Alexander: A History of the Persian Empire*. Translated by Peter T. Daniels. Winona Lake, IN: Eisenbrauns, 2002.

Campbell, Joseph. *The Masks of God: Occidental Mythology*. New York: Viking, 1964.

Cavendish, Richard, ed. *An Illustrated Encyclopedia of Mythology*. London: Orbis, 1980.

———. *Legends of the World*. New York: Barnes and Noble Books, 1989.

Choksy, Jamsheed. *Evil, Good, and Gender: Facets of the Feminine in Zoroastrian Religious History*. New York: Peter Lang, 2002.

Curtis, Vesta Sarkhosh. *Persian Myths*. Austin: University of Texas Press, 1993.

Ferdowsi, Abolqasem. *Shahnameh: The Persian Book of Kings*. Translated by Dick Davis. New York: Viking, 2006.

Foltz, Richard C. *Spirituality in the Land of the Noble: How Iran Shaped the World's Religions*. Oxford, England: OneWorld Publications, 2004.

Frye, Richard. *The History of Ancient Iran*. Munich, Germany: Beck, 1984.

Hinnells, John R. *Persian Mythology*. New York: Peter Bedrick, 1985.

Rahman, S. F., and J. Darmesteter, eds. and trans. *The Zend Avesta of Zarathustra: Selections*. 3rd ed. Sequim, WA: Holmes, 2005.

Weisehöfer, Josef. *Ancient Persia from 550 B.C. to 650 A.D.* Translated by Azizeh Azodi. New York: I. B. Taurus, 2004.

Zaehner, R. C. *The Dawn and Twilight of Zoroastrianism*. London: Phoenix Press, 1961.

NOTES *on* QUOTATIONS

Quoted passages in sidebars come from the following sources:

"The First Sin," page 38, from the *Bundahis* [or *Bundahishn*], translated by E. W. West, in *Pahlavi Texts*, Part I, vol. 5 of *Sacred Books of the East* (Oxford: Oxford University Press, ca. 1880), at http://www.sacred-texts.com/zor/sbe05/sbe0524.htm

"The Fall of Yima," page 57, from the *Zamyad Yasht* ("Hymn to the Earth"), translated by James Darmesteter, in *The Zend Avesta*, Part II, vol. 23 of *Sacred Books of the East* (Oxford: Oxford University Press, ca. 1882), at http://www.sacred-texts.com/zor/sbe23/sbe2324.htm#fr_1307

"The King of Birds," page 76, from *Shahnameh: The Persian Book of Kings* by Abolqasem Ferdowsi, translated by Dick Davis (New York: Viking, 2006).

"The End of Evil," page 85, from the *Denkard*, Book 7, translated by E. W. West, in vol. 5 of *Sacred Books of the East* (Oxford: Oxford University Press, 1897), at http://www.avesta.org/denkard/dk7.html#chap1

INDEX

Page numbers for illustrations are in boldface

Achaemenid Persian Empire, 17–19
Ahura Mazda (supreme deity), 23–24, 25, 27
  creation story, **30**, 31–37, **33**, **35**, **36**
  and king Yima, 52, 53–56
  Zarathustra and, 31, 79, 80, 83, **83**
Alexander the Great, 19
Angra Mainyu (evil spirit), 23–24, 31–37, **33**, **36**, 54, 56
Aryans, 17, 23, 24

Binder of Demons, 42, 48–49, **48**

creatures, mythical
  king of birds, 76–77, **76**
  mythical horse, **68**, 69–75, **71**, **72**, **73**, **74**
Cyrus the Great, 17

Darius I (king), 18–19, **18**, 24, **24**

Dughdhova (mother of Zarathustra), 81

Feraydun (Persian hero and king), 65–67, **67**, 71
Ferdowsi (poet), 41–42, 69
fire
  gift of, 46–47
  in Zoroastrian worship, 24–25, **26**, 27, **27**
first humans, **30**, 31–39, **33**, **35**, **36**, **38**
freemen and serfs, 22

gardens, **12**
geography, 13–14, **14**, **15**
good and evil
  battle between, 23–24, 27
  end of evil, 84, **84**
  path of evil, 61–63, **63**, **64**
  White Demon, 73–75, **73**, **74**
Greek conquest and culture, 19

Hushang (king), 42, 44–47, **47**

Iran, 13, 19, 24
Islam, 19, 24

94 | *The* **ANCIENT PERSIANS**

Jamshid (evil king), 59–60, 64

Kayumars (first mortal king), 42, 43–46, **43**
kings, nobles, and commoners, Persian, **20**, 21–22, **22**
  first Persian kings, **40**, 41–49, **43**, **45**, **47**, **48**, **49**
  king of the golden age, **50**, 51–57, **53**, **56**
  kings and triumphs over good and evil, **58**, 59–67, **63**, **64**, **65**, **67**

lower-class, Persian, 22, **22**

men, Persian, 22
Merdas (king), 61–62
middle-class, Persian, 22

palaces, Persian, **16**, 18
Parthians, 19

religion, fire in Zoroastrian worship, 24–25, **26**, 27, **27**
Rostam and His Mythical Horse, **68**, 69–75, **71**, **72**, **73**, **74**

Sassanian dynasty, 19, **19**, 24
Seleucid dynasty, 19

serfs, 22
Shahnameh (Ferdowsi), 41–42, 59, 69–70
slaves, Persian, 22

Tahmures (Binder of Demons), 42, 48–49, **48**

upper-class, Persian, 21–22

women, Persian, **10–11**, 22, **28**

Yima (king of the golden age), **50**, 51–57, **53**, **56**

Zahhak (serpent king), 59–60, 61–67
Zarathustra (prophet), 52
  birth of, 81
  life of, **78**, 79–80
  marvels and miracles of, 82–84, **82**, **83**, **84**
  teachings of, 23–24, **24**, 27, 31
Zoroastrianism, 24–25, **26**, 27, **27**, 41
  creation story, **30**, 31–37, **33**, **35**, **36**
  and the end of evil, 84, **84**
  founding of, 79–84

ABOUT *the* AUTHOR

VIRGINIA SCHOMP has written more than seventy books for young readers on topics including dinosaurs, dolphins, occupations, American history, and ancient cultures. Ms. Schomp earned a Bachelor of Arts degree in English Literature from Penn State University. She lives in the Catskill Mountain region of New York with her husband, Richard, and their son, Chip.